ALTERNATE SKIFFY

ALTERNATE SKIFFY

Edited by
Mike Resnick
and Patrick Nielsen Hayden

Wildside Press
Berkeley Heights, NJ ● 1996

ALTERNATE SKIFFY

An original publication of Wildside Press.

No portion of this book may be reproduced by any means, electronic or otherwise, without first obtaining the written permission of the publisher. For more information, contact:

Wildside Press
522 Park Avenue
Berkeley Heights, NJ 07922

First Edition

CONTENTS

INTRODUCTION #1

It's all Patrick's fault.

You see, he was the purchasing editor of the Alternate series for Tor. You know the books—*Alternate Presidents*, *Alternate Kennedys*, *Alternate Warriors*, *Alternate Outlaws*, and so on.

Problem is, Patrick likes to be begged. Or at least proposed to. And there are a limited number of viable Alternate books. And I hate thinking up viable Alternate book proposals.

So one night we were having dinner at a Worldcon, or perhaps it was a Nebula banquet, and the conversation went exactly as follows:

Mike: All right, then, how about *Alternate Diseases of the Big Toe*?

Patrick: Right or left?

Mike: Yes.

Patrick (after a thoughtful pause): I don't think so. Whether we chose the right or left toe, we'd alienate half our readership.

Mike: Okay, how about *Alternate Secretariat Tales*? In one he's a gelding, in another he's a milk horse, in a third he's magically transformed into the Lone Ranger's Silver...

Patrick: No, I hear Bantam is doing *Alternate Man o' War Stories*. This would be too close.

Mike: Okay, no way you can say no to this next one—what do you think of *Alternate Michael Jordans*? In one story, he could walk away from basketball in his prime and pursue a career as a minor league outfielder...

Patrick: Silliest thing I ever heard of. Forget it.

Mike: I give up. I can't think of any more Alternate skiffy stuff.

Patrick: That's it!!!

Mike (looking around quickly): What is, and how many legs has it got?

Patrick: That's the next Alternate book—*Alternate Skiffy*!

Mike: Oh, no! You're not sticking me with a book called *Alternate Skiffy*, and how much are you paying for it?

Patrick: I like it so much, I'll edit it with you, and we'll split the money.

So that's the story. Patrick is co-editing this volume because he is dead certain it'll enhance his reputation for editing Works of Quality. Me, I'm doing it for my half of the $108,350 advance that remains after shelling out a penny a word to all the writers. (It was too large a sum to fit on the contract, but he and Publisher John Betancourt promised that they'd remember it.)

Now Patrick's going to give you his version of an Introduction. Since I'm writing mine first, I have absolutely no idea what he's going to say, but if it differs in any detail, however slight, from my own, I'd advise you all to stand clear of him, because you never know which way he'll fall after God strikes him dead.

—Mike Resnick

INTRODUCTION #2

This is all Mike Resnick's fault. An enthusiastic newcomer to the dark lodge of SF editing, he has learned just enough of the lodge's mores—its *bushido*, if you will—to entrap the more conscientious.

An illustrative story (which is not about Mike Resnick, and thus will irritate him): Many years ago, during a late-night conversation at an SF convention, someone came up with a very silly idea for a theme anthology. "*True Tales of Sentient Food*," he said. (The reader will understand that this is not the actual silly idea proposed, but merely a representative idea possessing equivalent silliness.)

On hearing this, a dignified and much-honored writer of literary SF grew thoughtful. "Actually," he said slowly, "I can think of a story for that anthology."

Standing nearby was a respectable science fiction editor (i.e., not Mike Resnick), who laughed merrily and replied, "If you write it, I'll publish it!"

But no sooner were the words out of the editor's mouth than she realized, with dawning horror, what she had just done. *She had made an offer*... Ever since then, she has had to live with the knowledge that if that author ever writes that story (the reader will now understand why we did not wish to recall the actual anthology idea to anyone's memory), she will be obliged to publish that anthology, *no matter how stupid it is.*

Which brings me to the matter of Mike Resnick's proposals. *Alternate Presidents* begat *Alternate Kennedys*, which was followed by *Alternate Warriors*, which failed to preclude *Alternate Outlaws*. Never one to omit to beat an idea into the ground for lack of trying, Resnick then proposed *Alternate Alphabets* (too expensive to produce, especially with the bound-in decoder ring); *Alternate Base Numbers* ("Fahrenheit 111000011," big yawn); and *Alternate Sentient Food* (enough said). I turned these down with a light heart and a clear conscience.

"I can't believe you turned those down," said Resnick from behind the large monogrammed silk handkerchief with which he was affecting to dab away tears. "I need to come up with something that'll appeal to you *personally*."

"Sure," I replied, with what I thought was evident sarcasm. "I can see it now: *Alternate SF Editors*."

"Great idea!" shouted Resnick, grabbing my hand and shaking it vigorously before I could make my escape. "I'll do it!"

Goshwow neo he may be, but he understands far too much about editorial *bushido*. There is no help for it.

Welcome to *Alternate Skiffy*.

—Patrick Nielsen Hayden

Barry Malzberg is one of the true giants of this field, with more than 90 books to his credit—and to prove he hasn't lost his touch, he was nominated for both a Nebula and a Hugo in 1995. Here he writes about a science of the mind that was not created by L. Ron Hubbard and not published and promoted by John Campbell.

—M.R.

A SCIENCE OF THE MIND
Barry N. Malzberg

Dear Mr. Malzberg:

I'm going to turn over the papers but it's got to be with several qualifications. If you publish them in the projected Resnick anthology you are going to have to suppress my name and change the names of the correspondents . . . some of these people are still alive, all of them, living or dead, are vengeful (". . . the curse of Cthulhu will live forever!") and I want no repercussions. I do not even want in the preceding commentary to be referred to as a "leading commentator on science fiction" or a "first-rank fan historian" or a "long-term connisseur of the field" (although all of these are, of course, true, and there's more where that came from) because even *that* may be enough to implicate me amongst the shrewder members of First Fandom. Just say these papers fell into your hands from or amongst hands unidentified or unknown. Perhaps the full story as you insist *should* come out (although we have the full story on almost everything else and what has it gotten us but *All Our Yesterdays* and *The Immortal Storm* and later on the GEnie network) but it had better come out without *this* imprimatur, thank you very much.

Dear Ted:

This shows some promise but it's not the material I requested, not at all! You haven't gotten into the area of the birth trauma repressions as the cause of all neurosis and there's too much sex, too much talk about this or that kind of catharsis and all the stuff with the positions makes me very nervous. I run a family magazine here. I know it's 1951 and Freud has been dead for 12 years and Krafft-Ebing are household names down in Chelsea where you hang out

11

with the Hydra, but that doesn't do me any good and it doesn't help the readers.

What we need are a lot more engineering diagrams: Brain, hypothalamus, medulla oblongata as part of the "pistons of personality" as I put it to you, and the biological basis of sociopathy. Also, the one case history you have of the regressed sailor who re-enacted his birth is good but we need more of this. We need a great deal more! Ease up on the sex stuff and give me case histories showing the emotional basis of birth trauma, the pain and confusion which the sufferer feels and then how the methodology of regression and walk-through can take them back to the present. Also, I don't like "hermeneutics" as the name for the process. Okay, it's a kind of human engineering at which we're aiming but that name doesn't signify. Let's try something else. Diktonics? Frenetics? Well, no, frenetic is a word which has to do with excessive nervous energy which isn't the kind of tone we want to give this stuff, not exactly, but you'll come up with something. Take this back please and try to think it through.

❋

Dear Horace:

I'm utterly confused. I did this stuff to order, remember? We worked it out at the last Hydra meeting, don't you recall? The name "hermeneutics" was yours and you said, "Now, I want plenty of sex examples here, just make sure that you aren't *too* descriptive." Regression? You said that you would leave this up to me as long as the birth trauma stuff as a kind of original sin got placed right at the front. Okay, it was a *long* evening and you started to get nervous when Veronica came over and sat on your lap, but I don't think that this alone can explain the amnesia apparently afflicting your steel-trap mind. Case histories? You said as Veronica was snuggling your hair, "The trouble with all case histories, even Freud's, even the Wolf Man, is that they look faked, they read like something cooked up to make a point. You never read a case history which disagrees with a theory." So I held back on all of that stuff. Acutally, I'd prefer to give you case histories, they're the easiest thing for me to do, me with my sensitive, my "poetic" talent, my "compassionate heart" which you were so kind to enumerate and praise while Veronica was whispering ever more urgently into your shell-pink ear. You want case histories, I'll give you case histories. Just as long as you seem to think that the basic scheme is okay which you obviously should because it originated with you.

12

I am going to have to ask for some more money at this time, though. The two hundred dollar advance was appreciated but I had to go over 10,000 words here as you know and that's not even 2¢ a word and there's too much stuff ahead of me. I would hope that you could find yourself springing for at least another $200. Remember, circulation-building carries a price and I'm going to sign my own name to this stuff which for all I know will change the way the fans look at me forever. Of course, all in the course of science. Science fiction may be our life but science is our goal, as you so passionately averred as the evening dwindled.

❋

Dear Ted:

I'm sending another $100 but that's all I can offer until the article is delivered satisfactorily and it's out of my own pocket. We've already stretched this too far. I did not appreciate your remarks about Veronica; I am a married man, she was not in my lap but on the arm of my chair and our proximity had little to do with sex and altogether too much to do with her miserable collaborative novel which in deference to Murray who got jammed into this deal I am probably going to have to take.

What do you mean, case histories always looked faked? Krafft-Ebing and Rorshach lived on their case histories, Stanford-Binet evolved the entire theory of applied intelligence from their case history technique! I am not asking you to outrightly lie here, I am merely suggesting that you do not have to fully verify your field research if you understand what I am saying.

I am excited by the possibilities here, the evolution of a science in what is already in less than a year's time the most exciting magazine in the history of science fiction, but I detect a certain cynicism in your response. If you don't want to do this, Ted, there are plenty of people lined up behind you, eager to take the project and run with it. All right, we'll go back to "hermeneutics." If you feel uncomfortable with any part of this, then go back to that circus you keep on talking about when you get drunk and do some high-wire work. It doesn't matter a bit to me, Ted. Writers are sacred but they are nonetheless only vessels. Sacred vessels to be sure but instruments of design. I hope to get this into an early 1952 issue as you know, certainly no later than March, so please get to it.

Dear Horace:

Here is the second and I trust final draft of "Hermeneutics—The Evolution of a Science." You will note that there are *three* case histories here as well as a personal memoir by the writer. I have graphed the birth trauma through all of its latent and more evident manifestations and have suggested an objective measurement of the trauma depending upon codified responses to a word-association test. I have also furnished a time-line beginning with Aristotle, passing lightly through Hegel and Marx, touching for a fervid instant upon Freud and expiring gracefully in that flowering of "Hermeneutics—The Evolution of a Science" in the 3/52 issue of *Galaxy*. I am your servant & etc.

✻

Dear Ted:

Your letter managed to ignore the fact that you are three months overdue on this revision, also that 9,000 of its first 10,000 words are unchanged from the original draft and the 5,000 words you have now added are so poorly integrated that they read like a clumsy afterthought. The case histories here or what you dignify with the descriptive term "case histories" read as if they were cobbled together from the stream-of-consciousness of some of your Sixth Avenue bar companions. And that "timeline" which represents hermeneutics as the peak of western civilization . . . do you think you are being funny, Ted? Do you think that I am so stupid or so obsessed with this hobby-horse that I would ride it regardless of the contempt you've shown here? Hermeneutics is serious stuff, but beyond that, this is a circulation builder for a family magazine and it is the efficacy of the audience aspects which must be my primary concern. Do you think that I ever lost sight of this?

You think that you are smarter than the editors on whom you are dependent, that's the problem with so many of you, Ted; I had thought that it might be a little different in *your* case, after all, you've done some editing of your own and of course were working along with Lester on first reading over at the competition for a few years after the Bomb. In any case, this is nowhere near being publishable and you're going to have to start from the beginning, blend in the new with the old material, slide it around, and also do some charts

14

and graphs, not wacky timelines, which will show the *applicative* aspects of hermeneutics. That drops us out of the March issue and a pity, I had wanted it to balance off Veronica's unfortunate novel which I have to start running then, and we'll probably lose the summer as well. Maybe you could put that sailor in the Merchant Marine. More verisimilitude. I mean, that's your service, am I right?

❊

Dear Horace:

Not a work about money, I note to my amusement. (Well, "amusement" is not the work I am seeking. A lecture on the contempt writers feel for editors, completely wrongheaded that contempt of course, instructions on amalgamating material and drawing some "charts and graphs" and a request to finagle case histories but not a word about money. I'm almost a year and three drafts and 15,000 words into this thing and now I'm supposed to start all over again?

So much for that, Horace. I'm going to take the material elsewhere. You'll put me through one rewrite after the next, one bit of imperious dictatorship after the next with lectures on my inferiority and gratitude and then you'll dump the thing anyway. So this is goodbye. Didn't think I'd do it, did you? Thought that I needed the market so much for "my crap" as you so charitably put it one well-remembered night at Hydra that I'd put up with any humiliation but that just isn't the case. I'd rather ship out as a Merchant Marine or be a 34-year-old trapezist before I'd go through with more of this crap.

❊

Ted:

Not so fast, pal. This is *my* idea. Hermeneutics is *my* conception, I gave it to you, remember? It's assignment work. If you can't do it, if you can't do a professional job then that's your decision but it's not for you to take elsewhere. It's for me to take back. Which I do herewith. And the next round on Sixth Avenue is yours, that is if I see you first. In which case I won't see you and you're not up for a round either. Is that paradox too sophisticated for you?

❊

Horace:

How do you spell "overreaching." In any case, one drunk with an old pal and one mumbled word, "hermeneutics," doesn't make for what I would call provenance. I've already taken it to what you so charitably call the competition and I suggest that you bow out of this now because as you know, Horace, the competition has more pull at the distributors than you and your publisher combined and would be made very unhappy if you tried to make their lives difficult. Yours is a *new* magazine, remember? I've looked at the advance galleys of Veronica's collaboration, she showed them to me and I have to tell you, you don't need "balancing." You need about seventeen thousand gallons of white paint.

Dear Sturgeon:

Thanks for sending over this essay on "hermeneutics" which I agree would be a real challenge, a real reach for the readers although that stuff with the sailor kicking the stomachs would definitely have to go. In any case, I can't use it; as you know we've been more than dabbling with something similar in the past couple of years and I think it's time to lay low on this issue for a while. The fans aren't ready for it and if *they* aren't, neither is the world. Veronica tells me that you might be ready to start with fiction again, I'd be happy to see it. (She seems mad at you for some reason, too.) In forty years the situation may look entirely different but right now I have to tell you I just see no future in this kind of stuff.

Have you tried Gold with it? Maybe he'll feel differently with his keen market sense (Heh-heh.)

—Campbell

Frederik Pohl has worn many hats in SF: editor, writer, agent, fan. Here he returns to his role as historian, to chronicle the role played by Astounding Science Fiction—*and its hard-driving, charismatic editor—during SF's "Golden Age."*

—P.N.H.

THE GOLDEN YEARS OF "ASTOUNDING"
by Frederik Pohl

When we speak of the "Golden Age of Science Fiction" the time we generally mean is the period from the late 1930s through the war and post-war years of the 1940s, when *Astounding Science Fiction* was the clear leader of the science-fiction field. It was more than that. It can be argued that what happened in that magazine in those years essentially defined what science fiction was all about, not just then but for all time to come . . . and yet it could have been quite different.

Before that Golden Age began, *Astounding* in fact had had a rather unpromising history. It was inaugurated in 1930 by the Clayton group of pulp magazines because, it was said, the publisher needed an extra title to make the gang-printing of the color covers economical. It survived only a little over two years. Bought up by the pulp colossus of Street & Smith in a sort of fire sale of the Clayton assets in 1933, the magazine was given to one of Street & Smith's staff editors, F. Orlin Tremaine, to make of it what he would.

What that was to be was not well defined. Tremaine was a competent pulp editor, well experienced in the crime, Western and adventure fields. Science fiction, however, was terra incognita to him, and after a few years of tinkering and experimentation he decided to seek as his replacement someone with direct experience in that perplexing area. He chose a young writer, the son of a telephone company engineer, John W. Campbell, Jr.

It was perhaps inevitable that whoever became the editor of *Astounding* in that period would dominate the development of the science-fiction field. At that time there was essentially no such thing as book publication for science fiction in America— apart from a

17

handful of juveniles, the American science-fiction novels published in the 1930s can be counted almost on the fingers of one hand—and there were only three magazines in the field. Among them, *Astounding* held all the cards. It appeared every month—its competitors were bi-monthly; it paid twice as well as the others in the field—a full penny a word; and it paid promptly, while the others paid only on publication, and sometimes seemed reluctant to pay their writers at all. Any writer who was concerned about his income—as most Americans were very deeply, in those years of the Great Depression—quickly saw that *Astounding* was the market to aim for, and so its editor, whoever he was, was almost certain to have first pick of everything written in the field. Opportunity knocked for young John Campbell, and he gave every indication of readiness to seize it.

❄

In those years the headquarters of Street & Smith was at the corner of Seventh Avenue and West 17th Street, in the Chelsea district of New York City. The ramshackle structure that housed the company was not a single building. It was composed of several old edifices that had been thrown together to meet the needs of the publisher.

The Seventh Avenue side was given over to the giant rotary printing presses that turned out each month's issues. When those presses were running, which was usually, the noise reached every part of the structure, while the thudding of the binding machines rattled the windows. Because of the huge rolls of newsprint paper waiting to be fed to the presses, the entire complex had been designated a fire hazard by the city authorities. Smoking was banned throughout the structures.

It was Campbell's bad luck that he was an addicted, and stubborn, cigarette smoker.

It was inevitable that he would be caught, although he took precautions. He arranged with receptionists, secretaries and editorial assistants to set up a telephone warning service, to notify him when the fire marshals were inspecting the buildings. Generally the system worked, but there were slips. The first time Campbell was caught with a burning cigarette in the little rectangular copper ashtray on his desk he was let off with a warning; the second time he had to pay a $10 fine; the third time was worse. This time the fine was larger, and the company of Street & Smith was fined as well.

When Campbell left the office that day his card was missing from the rack by the time clock at the employees' entrance. Instead there was a pink slip to notify him that his services were no longer required.

Street & Smith began an instant talent search, and within three weeks had located Campbell's replacement; not an issue was skipped. The man they chose was a twenty-four-year-old New York fan who had sold one or two science-fiction stories and edited a number of science-fiction "fan mags," as well as having functioned as an editor of the semi-professional *Fanciful Tales of Space and Time*. But perhaps his most important qualification was that Donald Allen Wollheim was a confirmed, almost an obsessive, non-smoker.

He was also a thoroughly schooled student of science fiction, who had definite opinions on what could be done in the field—and, as we shall see, he began to put them into practice at once.

❋

When we look at the honor roll of the writers who have shaped modern science fiction, it is startling to realize how many of them first burst into prominence in that one magazine, under that one editor, in that single brief period of three years, from 1938 through 1941. L. Ron Hubbard, C. M. Kornbluth, Ray Bradbury, Tennessee Williams, Theodore Sturgeon, Robert W. Lowndes, Isaac Asimov and many others were actually first published there and then; others who had had relatively minor previous careers now attained new heights of skill and success in that period. And even the already famous sometimes became more famous still.

Perhaps the outstanding example of that is the case of Edgar Rice Burroughs. Although the creator of Tarzan and the author of the John Carter Mars novels was already world-famous (and indeed quite wealthy, owing to his prudent early investments in the waste-lands that are now the thriving community of Tarzana), yet he had not published a "Barsoom" story in a science-fiction magazine since the days of the *Amazing Stories Annual*. He had become marginalized in the mainstream of the rapidly booming science-fiction audience, and it was Wollheim's serialization of *Synthetic Men of Mars* in 1940 and *Llana of Gathol* in the year following that earned Burroughs a new fan audience and led directly to the famous series of Barsoom movies starring Buster Crabbe as John Carter and the young Olivia de Haviland as his Dejah Thoris.

What Wollheim could do for a promising, but as yet almost unknown, writer is exemplified by the middle-aged South African, become an Oxford don, whom Wollheim recruited to his stable early in 1939.

Wollheim was something of an Anglophile. As a fan he had always made a point of keeping abreast of what was happening abroad. As a result he was familiar with the work of a number of promising English writers; that was how S. Fowler Wright (*The Spider's War*, published in *Astounding* in 1942) and W. Olaf Stapledon (*Sirius*, 1943) were added to his list of contributors.

But Stapledon and Wright had substantial publishing credits already, although mostly in England, and their works were clearly science fiction.

That could not be said of the short English children's story Wollheim read and admired in 1937; it dealt with elves and gnomes of untraditional kinds, but in this unpromising juvenile Wollheim saw the germ of a major science-fiction writer. The Oxford don responded quickly to Wollheim's invitation to write for *Astounding* and gladly accepted Wollheim's editorial suggestions. The result began to appear in 1942, as the first of a series of novelettes of the "Middle World" of the planet Saturn.

Scientifically these "Middle World" stories were dubious even in 1942 (and are preposterous now, when it is clear that Saturn can have no such solid body), but their beautifully imagined details and heart-warming affirmations of the virtues of goodness and loyalty gave each of them a clear first place in *Astounding*'s Analytical Laboratory. Their popularity remained so great that even the trade book publishers, previously openly hostile to science fiction of any kind, soon perceived that they represented an attractive new marketing category, and so the novelettes were promptly gathered into the famous *Lord of Saturn's Rings* novel which once and for all made the reputation of John R.R. Tolkien.

It was too late for Wollheim to do anything of the sort for the man who was perhaps his most admired writer of all, Howard P. Lovecraft, since Lovecraft had died just months before Wollheim became editor of *Astounding*. However, Wollheim was always resourceful. It happened that F. Orlin Tremaine had actually published two of

Lovecraft's works, *The Shadow Out of Time* and *At the Mountains of Madness*, in *Astounding* during his tenure in 1936. The response of the readers had been good, and Wollheim was determined to find some way of continuing the works of the late master. He found the right man to take up the torch of Lovecraft's work in his old friend (and fellow member of the New York Futurian Society) Robert W. Lowndes.

Lowndes was then twenty-two years old and, apart from some short poems, had not yet achieved professional publication anywhere. He was, however, almost as great an admirer of Lovecraft's work as Wollheim himself. Lowndes had struck up a friendship with the aging master and had even been given Lovecraft's gracious permission to write stories of his own in "the Cthulhu Mythos", as the Lovecraft canon was called. He began doing so for Wollheim at once, and Lowndes's first Cthulhu story, "A Martian Necronomicon", appeared in the first issue of *Astounding* which was composed entirely of Wollheim's purchases. Sadly, that first story was not a great success. The readers found the mixture of Elder Gods and Doc Smith-like atomic-powered spaceships more confusing than delightful. That might have discouraged a lesser writer; to Lowndes it was merely a challenge. With his revision and completion of Lovecraft's unfinished manuscript, *The Dream-Quest of Unknown Kadath*, a year later Lowndes hit his stride and his touch never faltered again. Each of the subsequent seven Lovecraft-Lowndes novels rated high with the readers when they were published as serials in *Astounding*, and are still in print as novels, with an aggregate worldwide sale, including translations, of many millions of copies. As the English critic, Kingsley Amis, wrote in his landmark academic study of science fiction, *New Horrors from Hell*, "Lowndes clearly out-Lovecrafted Lovecraft with his eldritch visions of those unforgettable partly squamous, partly rugose Shamblers from Beyond."

The Futurian Society, indeed, was an untapped lode of talent for Wollheim. Dedicated fans bursting with the ambition to become pros, more than a dozen of the Futurians appeared in his magazine within those first few years. A few of the Futurians made their mark as artists, including Hannes Bok, Boris Dolgov and Leslie Perri; one, John B. Michel, became a distinguished editor, first as Wollheim's assistant and then going on to a career of his own elsewhere. But it

21

was the Futurian writers who are best remembered. Among them were C.M. Kornbluth, James Blish, Damon Knight, Isaac Asimov (and, of course, the undersigned.)

Wollheim had one other major source for finding new talent: the slush pile. Of course, every editor has this at his disposal, for the "slush pile" is nothing more than the accumulation of unsolicited manuscripts the mailman delivers in volume every business day; but Wollheim's eye was keener than most. Out of the slush he picked Theodore Sturgeon, Henry Kuttner, and Ray Bradbury, to name only a few of those major writers whose first sales were to Wollheim's *Astounding*.

Not all of Wollheim's discoveries went on to major careers; some he recalled later as great disappointments. The young Southern writer Tennessee Williams, for instance, came out of the slush pile (though in fact he had sold one earlier story, to *Weird Tales*.) Wollheim found Williams's sardonic, biting anti-Utopias of future Amazonian dictatorships brilliantly written and published all he could get, and was chagrined when the young author left the field for other interests. "Williams could have been another Kuttner," Wollheim said later, "if he hadn't wasted himself trying to break into that rat's nest, the Broadway theater." Robert A. Heinlein was another who wandered away; when Wollheim found "Lifeline" in the slush he predicted a great future for the retired naval officer; but, as Wollheim put it afterwards, "The man was just lazy. He only wrote when he needed the money for something, and he had his Navy pension." Even more of a loss, in Wollheim's view, was the dashing young L. Ron Hubbard, whose *Final Blackout* was one of the most popular serials of 1940; but when Hubbard went off prospecting for diamonds, and found them, he gave up writing completely.

Wollheim was never one to throw out the baby with the bathwater; in his housecleaning he was careful to preserve the best of the writers inherited from his predecessors. So L. Sprague de Camp, Jack Williamson, Eando Binder, Edward E. Smith, Ph.D., and many others remained stalwarts in *Astounding* throughout all their long lives.

But it was the newcomers that made Wollheim's reputation—and their own; and that is why the "Golden Age of Wollheim" remains a watershed in the history of science fiction, unlikely ever to be matched again.

❋

It may be of interest, in closing this essay, to look at what became of Wollheim's predecessors. Tremaine, who had voluntarily abdicated his editorship in favor of John Campbell, soon left Street & Smith to start his own pulp-magazine publishing company; he was reasonably successful, until ill health forced him into early retirement.

John Campbell, of course, went on to a brilliant writing career in *Amazing Stories* under the successive editorships of Ray Palmer and Howard V. Browne, where he published the stories based on his famous "Three Laws of Robotics" and his celebrated classic novel of an Earth surrounded by Venus-like clouds, "The Night the Stars Came Out". These are still rated by aficionados of the field as among the best-loved science-fiction stories of all time. Campbell's controversial later works—particularly his story-a-month contributions to the *Amazing* of the 1950s dealing with psionics, Deros, saucer people, the Hieronymus Machine and the Dean Drive—have tarnished his reputation in some circles, but there is no doubt they were commercially wildly successful, as indeed they remain today.

Interviewed shortly before his death in 1971, Campbell expressed complete satisfaction with his career. Fitting a cigarette into his long holder, he waved it at the reporter. "This cigarette was the best friend I ever had," he declared. "Smoking these things saved me from making a terrible mistake with my life. Wollheim was the right man for the job at *Astounding*. He had the temperament to sit behind an editorial desk all his life, and I just didn't."

*Tony Lewis has not only sold a batch of stories, but also chaired the 1971
Worldcon, the first of the great Boston worldcons. Here he presents us with our
founding father, Hugo Gernsback, not as the penny-pinching publisher of a pulp
magazine, but as President of the League of Nations.*

—M.R.

PLUS ULTRA
Anthony R. Lewis

The Great War and What Came After, 1921

Hugo Gernsback glanced at his watch. There was ample time
to pack and catch the zeppelin to Geneva. He gazed about his office,
the office of the Prime Minister of Luxembourg, his eyes stopping
at the one framed photograph upon the wall. It showed some soldiers
in drab uniforms, standing in front of a landship. They held up a
captured German flag and smiled for the camera. He was one of those
soldiers, but it was not apparent to any innocent viewer. That had
been Berlin in late 1916; this was Luxembourg in 1921. Hugo
Gernsback was going to speak at a plenary meeting of the League of
Nations.

At the Luftschiffplatz, the sight of the zeppelin reminded him
of earlier days. He repeated an old story to his secretary. "Defeating
the Germans was easier than dealing with the Allied High Command.
Well, they're safely pensioned off along with their counterparts in
the Central Powers." He remembered the landships ("tanks" the
British had coded them) arrived in France in September 1916. The
brass wanted to use them as self-contained artillery pieces, but
Colonel Hugo Gernsback, Luxembourg volunteer seconded to the
B.E.F. had seen the technology to win the war.

After they had cracked the hard shell of the Hun, the drive to
Berlin and the Kaiser's order of surrender was a matter of weeks. Then
came the medals—the Croix de Guerre, Knight Commander of the
Most Excellent Order of the British Empire, and l'Ordre Grand
Ducal de la Couronne de Chene of Luxembourg. Peace brought a
seat in parliament, the Science Ministry, and then the Prime Minis-
tership of the Grand Duchy.

His secretary carried their luggage aboard the zeppelin *Goethe*. *She* lifted quietly, the nonflammable helium in her balloon floating them skywards. Her engines revved as she turned for Geneva.

✻

The League: Geneva, 1930

Hugo Gernsback had been President of the League of Nations since 1926. The last few years had been successful. Speaking to the American President Hoover as one engineer to another, he was able to convince that worthy to bring the U.S. into the League. (Everyone knew it was Gernback's address to the Senate that brought about ratification of the High Covenant.)

It was time to address the Assembly. Earth was mostly at peace and it was time to push outward into the vaster universe that surrounded mankind. He would call for the creation of an International Science Council, a group removed from politics, answering only to the higher ethical imperatives. The core of the League, the European states, were ready. The British had been dubious but the promise to build the rocket base in British East Africa had won them over. The Americans were interested, but he doubted their Congress would spend money on anything outside their own borders.

"M. le President," his Austrian executive secretary said politely. "It is time to address the Assembly on your great task. How wonderful—today, the world; tomorrow, the universe."

"Thank you, Adolf," he responded and arose to take the future of mankind away from the leaders of the past.

✻

The Rocket Base: British East Africa, 1938

It was early morning north of Mombasa. The sun was rising from the Indian Ocean, casting its particular equatorial light upon the structures of the League's ISC Rocket Base. The ceremonies, naming the base for the deceased rocket pioneer K. E. Tsiolkovsky, were a week in the past. The confusion connected to that event explained the current problem—two important visits were scheduled simultaneously. Stanley Weinbaum, the world's foremost SR editor, was being given the grand tour in return for his continued support of the space program in his magazine. The copies of *Epiphenomenal* around the base were no Potemkin village. Most of the technical staff were subscribers. Some tried to write the stuff. More importantly,

25

Hugo Gernsback would arrive the same day. Though he no longer held any official League position, his prestige was immense; no one wanted to offend him.

That's just what Robert Goddard said to Hermann Oberth: "Hermann, no one in the space program wants to offend Uncle Hugo."

"Of course not, Robert. But this is a not-sufficiently-to-be-damned situation, is it not? Do we arrange separate tours or put them together? How will our elder statesman deal with a young SR writer? *Ach, antworten Sie mich,*" he sighed.

"Put them together, I'd say. They may have more in common than one might think. I understand that Gernsback tried his hand at writing SR, before there was any SR. Dreadful, I understand. It's a good thing he decided to go into politics instead of trying to be a writer."

"Jawohl, let Werner take them around."

Werner von Braun was newly come to Tsiolkovsky Rocket Base from the Hebrew University of Entebbe. There he had studied rocketry and aeronautical engineering under some of the greatest minds of the time—men and women who had emigrated to the Jewish homeland that the British had established in Uganda following the Great War. His wife was setting up their apartment. Later that month, they would visit her family in Mombasa where her father was Chief Rabbi. But for now, he was nervous. He had to lead his two greatest idols through the rocket base. He was responsible for both Hugo Gernsback and Stanley Weinbaum.

He need not have worried. Although the two had never met before, they fell into the sort of argument that only good friends can have.

"No, no, Herr Weinbaum. It is the scientific extrapolation that gives value to speculative romance. The story, if anything, is secondary to that."

"But, Herr Gernsback, without a story, one might as well be writing a scientific paper."

"Yes, that is what SR should be—a scientific paper in narrative form. I understand the need to sugar-coat the bitter pill. The average man—and woman, too, I daresay—in the street still looks upon science with deep suspicion as a vicious ogre that constantly upsets and disarranges his life and habits."

"Yes, but . . ."

"And, what is more, the scientists and engineers are rapidly catching up to you SR writers. Many of your predictions have already come to pass—liquid fertilizer, wide-spread use of coin-operated vending machines, precision aquatic dancing, radio-vision, the actinoscope. I warn you fellows—get on the ball or we will overtake you. In my lifetime, we'll be landing on the Moon; that will do in a number of your stories, won't it?"

"Those particular stories, yes—but the universe is larger than the Moon and man's mind can be larger than the universe . . ."

The argument continued in a pleasant manner until late afternoon. Gernsback excused himself. He had to rest, for the next day he was off by the zeppelin *Shakespeare* to the Union of South Africa. There he would oversee the League Plebiscite, requested by the KwaZulu, to abolish the present bilingualism and replace it with one common tongue—German.

The Space Station: Supra-Africa Orbit, 1952

Hugo Gernsback floated through the tunnel connecting the Earth-to-orbit shuttle *Tesla* with the League's first space station, the *E. E. Hale*. He had caught a brief glimpse of the rotating wheel from the shuttle's porthole. The sun was shining off the white ceramic tiles that gave the wheel its nickname, *The Brick Moon*. He was helped through the airlock by a tall black man, probably a Maasai, Gernsback thought.

"Welkommen zum Weltraum," he greeted the Luxemburger in his Afrikan-Deutsch.

"How it would have startled Europeans of the last century," Gernsback thought, "to find so many men, and even women, of colour working on such highly technical projects." As his guide, an Oberleutnant in the Kaiserliche Weltraumflotte by his insignia, led him to his temporary lodgings, he wondered just what it was about Deutsche Kultur that made it possible to bring whole nations from savagery to civilization in less than two generations. He thought, "Most Germans believed that everyone wanted to be German and would work hard to achieve that status. Possibly true." He had been present at the ceremonies when his native Luxembourg had joined New Federal German Empire.

"Herr Gernsback, we have given you a room with a view of the

27

Jules Verne. The Commandant thought you would like that."

"*Dankesehr, Herr Oberleutnant. Und danken Sie der Kommandant fur mich.*" He moved cautiously under the low gravity created by the centrifugal force of the spinning wheel. His room was at the rim and as he looked out the porthole, parallel to the axis of rotation, he could see, apparently spinning in the opposite direction, the Moonship. He would only visit it this trip, but he would be on it when it cast free from the Cradle of Mankind (as Tsiolkovsky had put it) and wended its way to the cold face of the Moon. He would be on that ship. Nothing was more certain.

❋

The Moon: Landing and Aftermath, 1955

It was August 10, 1955 and the *Jules Verne* was in circumlunar orbit. Gernsback looked out the triply-glazed window at the pitted surface, now so close. He turned, placed the space helmet upon his head and joined it to the rest of the suit with a telepneumo locking device. He passed into the tunnel leading to the *Robert Goddard*, the ship that would land upon the Moon. It was named after America's leading rocket scientist, who had died ten years ago to this very date.

The lander pitched and yawed. He could see the microminiaturized valves and relays of the artificial brain that guided the ship to the Lunar surface. The crew all wore spacesuits in the vacuum which made it unnecessary to enclose any of the individual valves in glass. Soon, with a slight jolt, the cushioned legs took up the landing momentum transfer and then all was still.

The Captain filled the cabin with air. After all had removed their helmets, Gernsback unsealed his personal bag and removed a bottle of champagne. "Gentlemen, this calls for a toast." They all grinned at him and removed appropriate glasses from their packs. Apparently, his secret had not been all that well-kept.

After the toast, the Captain turned to him, "Herr Gernsback, the crew have decided that the honour of being the first of our race, the human race, to set foot upon a supramundane body must belong to you who for so long this project nurtured have." His attempted protest was shouted down by the multinational crew, representing all the great divisions of humanity.

Once on the surface, he scanned the horizon. Above his head was the Earth in partial phase—a blue world speckled with clouds.

"How beautiful, and how small and fragile it looks." He took the League flag, painted upon metal foil—for there was no air here to unfurl it—spread it out and forced the pointed staff into the Lunar surface. "I claim this Moon for all mankind in the name of the League of Nations and the International Science Council for use in eternal peace."

On Earth, there was universal euphoria. Nation after nation declared August 10 to be a holiday—the First Day of the New Era of Mankind. Radio-vision reporters dragooned SR writers to explain to the masses just what this event meant. Unfortunately, during all the interviews, the same question arose: "Just what will you fellows write about now that we've landed on the Moon?"

In Paris, Charles Henneberg challenged his interviewer to a duel for such an insult to the literature of Jules Verne.

In Moscow, Isaac Asimov instantly composed a poem reducing his interviewer to silence. Asimov then gave a two-hour impromptu on Konstantin Eduardovitch Tsiolkovsky.

In New York, Stanley Weinbaum solemnly and carefully told his interviewer that the Moon was only a small part of the universe and that true SR adventures lay within the mind.

In St. Louis, Robert Heinlein politely but firmly told his interviewer that extrapolating human interactions and not locales were what made SR stories so important.

And in Boston, Prof. John W. Campbell, faculty advisor to the M.I.T.S.R.C., earnestly told his interviewer that the major function of SR was to educate and interest people in science. "It was not primarily intended to entertain or to amuse ."

The Global Congress of Speculative Romance: Africa Again, 1963

Late October in 1963 and the Global Congress of Speculative Romance had convened in Nairobi. The eminent Russian SR writer and palaeontologist Ivan Antonovich Yefremov was the Guest of Honour. This year sadness overlay the usual festivities of SR "fandom." The great Stanley G. Weinbaum, author of many classic stories—and, for many years, editor of *Epiphenomenal Speculative Romance*—had died peacefully in his sleep at the age of 63. The SR world mourned. His successor at the magazine, Keith Hamilton, Ph.D., proposed that the Glocon present a set of awards for the best

SR stories of the year, in Weinbaum's memory. To the official name, SR Achievement Award, was instantly appended the nickname "Stanley", by analogy to the motion picture awards. The program staff, headed by young Cincinnati fan Michael D. Resnick, had staged a coup and convinced Weinbaum's old friend, former League President Hugo Gernsback to present the inaugural prizes.

As Gernsback mounted to the podium, the hall rang with loud plaudits to the man who, more than anyone else, had made space travel possible. After this lengthy standing ovation, a great hush fell upon the assembly as they took their seats and followed the printed text in the copies of the speech that had been distributed.

"My friends," he began. "I knew Stanley Weinbaum for a quarter of a century. We first met, not far from here, at the Tsiolkovsky Rocket Base . . ." He went on and on, detailing Weinbaum's contributions with many references and the occasional self-conscious multi-lingual pun. He praised the scientific manner in which Weinbaum had presented his stories. He reinforced and supported the committee's decision to issue the Speculative Romance Achievement Awards. But here he broke with the committee.

"As I told Stanley Weinbaum in 1937, we must always be out ahead of the present because the present is rolling us up from behind. And it is in the honour of Stanley Weinbaum that I suggest that the term 'Speculative Romance' has outlived its usefulness. I propose that a new name be found for SR. And that this body be the first to adopt it."

After explaining what was wrong with SR—notably the lack of scientific rigor in "speculative" and the unfortunate confusion between the original meaning of "romance" as a story and its present connection with overly sentimental love stories, he continued. "Now let us look into the elements of an acceptable substitute term. SR—under any term or name—must, in my opinion, deal first and foremost in futures. It must, in story form, forecast the wonders of man's progress to come. That also means distant exploits and explorations of space and time." He paused, drank from his water, and continued, finishing with a suggested list—Predifiction, Futufiction, Prophiction, and Telefiction. "I rather like that last one, but, in honour of those who have gone before, ladies and gentlemen, I submit for your approval—SCIENCE FICTION."

❋

Legal Notice

Glocon, Global Congress of Speculative Romance, Global Speculative Romance Circle, GSRC, Speculative Romance Achievement Award, and Stanley Award are service marks of the Global Speculative Romance Circle, an unincorporated literary society.

Brian Thomsen created the Questar line at Warner Books, before moving off into the hinterlands to run TSR, Inc.'s book line. During that time he also wrote about a dozen stories, most of them featuring his continuing character, Mouse Marlowe. For this book, he gives us a totally different yet oddly familiar Julius Shwartz, who in our universe edited Batman for half a century.

—M.R.

OSCAR NIGHT AT SWIFTY'S
by Brian M. Thomsen

From *Variety Sunday Supplement*
March 28, 1993

After the film clips, presentations, and plugs of the Academy Awards Ceremony itself, the "in-place to see-and-be-seen" among both the current and classic stars of the motion picture community is without a doubt the annual after-hours party at the palatial home of superstar, fast-track Hollywood agent Julius "Swifty" Schwartz.

Schwartz, a member of the Hollywood community for over fifty years, is still recognized as the king of the deal makers despite his semi-retirement. Anyone who is anyone has at one time or another been involved in a "Swifty" Schwartz package, and Monday night's festivities will undoubtedly be overflowing with wine, women, songs, and, of course, deal-making.

Schwartz began his deal-making career in New York City during the 1930s where he established himself as the first literary agent to deal exclusively in horror, science fiction, and fantasy, a segment of the overall literary marketplace that was considered at the time to be far beneath the standards of most reputable agents, and usually relegated to the venues of the newsstand pulps. During these early years, he quickly established himself as an agent with an eye for talent, representing such then-neophyte authors as Ray Bradbury, Robert Bloch, Alfred Bester, Leigh Brackett, and Otto Binder (and those were only the Bs!). Then, in 1943, happily married, with a family on the way, he decided to set his sights on bigger game and went west to Hollywood, where the resident industry was already bringing fantasy to life.

His early years in Hollywood were largely spent pitching what he called "superhero" screenplays to the major studios. The then terrifying shadow of the Axis powers loomed over America, and in Schwartz's own words, "the people needed heroes with powers and abilities that exceeded those of the average Joe on the street. How they got their powers didn't matter (they could even have been born on another planet). As long as they didn't have a foreign accent, the American movie-goer would gobble them up." Most of these early scripts were made into low budget, contract player serials that proved to be quite successful with the Saturday matinee crowds.

Once the war was over Schwartz landed his first feature deal with Universal for a film adaptation of a story he had sold to the pulps when he was in New York. The film was directed by James Whale and proved an immediate hit, spawning an immediate frenzy for all of the author's previous works, driving them to bestsellerdom despite the author's untimely death ten years before. The film went on to inspire the most successful cinematic horror series of all time.

Schwartz says, "I only wish Lovecraft could have been around to taste some of his success. As I sat there at the opening of *At the Mountains of Madness*, I thought to myself that he would have been proud." He then added, "However, even he would have tired of the series by the slasher versions of the 1970s. Not even I could sit through the last films in the series, *The Mountains of Madness Have Eyes* and *Hercules and Santo in the Haunted Lands that Exist Beyond the Mountains of Madness*, and *Mad Mountain Rock*."

The success of the Lovecraft series established Schwartz as *the* agent to have. In the words of Ed Hamilton, "The feeling was that if he could do such an outstanding job with a dead author's work, there was no telling what he could do with a live one . . . but Julie didn't let success go to his head and continued to represent his previous clients from the New York days. Rumor has it that he turned down representing Sturges and Capra because he was afraid that he would neglect the other clients on his list."

1953 brought Schwartz his greatest success to date when he convinced George Pal to direct a film version of yet another deceased client's work, namely the now famous *A Martian Odyssey*, by Stanley G. Weinbaum. The screenplay by Ed Hamilton and Leigh Brackett went on to win the Academy Award that year and clearly established the science fiction genre as worthy of critical attention and cinematic success. "We weren't just making movies for the Saturday matinee crowds any longer," Schwartz said.

The sixties saw Schwartz diversifying, representing actors and directors as well as writers. He is credited with turning around the careers of many stars who had begun to suffer the strains of typecasting, including landing Marilyn Monroe the role of Gertrude in David Lean's *Hamlet* (for which she won her first Academy Award), and James Dean the role of Montag in *Fahrenheit 451*, and introducing Alfred Hitchcock to Alfred Bester, thus resulting in their collaborations on the two most successful science fiction pictures of all time, *The Demolished Man* and *The Stars My Destination*.

The seventies saw Schwartz establishing his agency as the foremost motion picture packager of all time. He finally turned over the actual representation of his stable to some of the younger associates in his employ in order to take on larger projects for the major studios.

"This allowed me to pick and choose a few projects a year that I could devote my time to while also giving me the chance to just sit around and play with my grandchildren," says Schwartz. Among the projects he oversaw during these years were the *Silver John* TV series and *The Ray Palmer Story*.

Schwartz's Oscar night get-togethers started in the 1950s. The first was held impromptu to celebrate Ray Bradbury's Oscar for the screenplay to *Moby Dick*. From then on it became an annual event because, in Schwartz's words, "It was a great excuse to sit around with old friends who you usually only get to see once a year." Hollywood insiders, however, have always alluded to the number of deals that originate at these affairs.

"The party is fun," said Otto Binder, "but the real excitement takes place in Julie's study. It's off-limits to everyone by the old crowd. It's Julie's star chamber."

Binder hastily added, "and no one in the star chamber calls him Swifty. That's strictly for the neophytes."

When asked what was in store for this year's party, Schwartz replied, "Oh, just fun for all."

And in the star chamber, "You'll find out soon enough."

From *Daily Variety*
April 13, 1993

It was revealed today that BMT, Inc., through its Warner Bros. film division, have just successfully acquired the rights to the *Skywalker* comic book series, from series creator and comic book publisher George Lucas. Lucas's representative on the deal, Julius "Swifty" Schwartz, claimed that it was financially the biggest deal of his illustrious career, and believed that it might very well start a trend in the motion picture industry to, perhaps, bring other comic book characters to life on the silver screen.

Linda Dunn has sold about a dozen stories, many to major markets, since breaking into print less than two years ago. One of her heros is Fritz Leiber, who in this alternate universe remained an actor rather than becoming a writer, and managed to land a most interesting part.

—M.R.

FRITZ LEIBER, ACTOR EXTRAORDINAIRE
Linda J. Dunn

Fritz Leiber paced nervously near the telephone. "Ring, damn it!"

Jonquil carried her drink into the room. "What are you so nervous about? It's just another job."

"Just another job?" Fritz turned around to glare at her. "This is the first chance I've had in years to play a part where I didn't have to wear some stupid space suit."

He groaned softly and rubbed his forehead. "I haven't been able to land a decent role since *The Day the Earth Stood Still.*"

"You can hardly blame me for that. I told you it was a bad decision." She shrugged. "It's still not too late. You could always leave Hollywood and go back to writing—"

"I'm an actor, not a writer," Fritz said. "Don't try to make me into something I'm not."

Jonquil drained the last drop of wine before speaking. "I'd rather be married to a poor writer than a rich actor who tries to bed all his co-stars."

Fritz sighed heavily. Jonquil stopped trusting him when he and Anne Francis made headlines during *Forbidden Planet.* It was just a publicity stunt but Jonquil trusted gossip columnists more than her own husband. Sometimes he wondered if he shouldn't just give up and—

The phone rang and he spun around to stare at it.

"Aren't you going to answer the phone?" Jonquil asked as she started forward.

Fritz waved her aside. "I'll get it myself." Taking a deep breath, he reached for the receiver.

"Hello?"

"Such a deal I got for you!" Marty laughed as Fritz let out a sigh of relief.

"I got the part?"

"Yeah. Roddenberry wanted some young punk who appeared in one of his other productions. Fortunately, the studio honchos agreed with me. The audience would never buy the idea of someone that young making Captain. We made him the science officer."

Fritz felt tears rolling down his cheeks.

"I'll send the script over by courier today," Marty said.

"Thanks," Fritz said. "I'll never forget you for this."

Marty laughed. "Save the thanks for later, after you see the script."

Fritz leaned against the table as he laid the receiver back into the cradle.

"You got the part?" Jonquil asked.

He turned around and smiled. "Yes. I play a ship's captain. Each week, we stop in a different port and explore some new place. I hope we get to do some location shooting."

"Can I go with you?"

Fritz sighed. "You still don't trust me?"

Jonquil laughed and shook her head. "Of course not. Who's the female lead?"

Fritz smiled. "Roddenberry's wife."

"How trusting of him," she said as she poured a drink for herself then held out a second glass. "Shall we celebrate?"

He shook his head. "You know I don't drink any more."

She laughed. "Just because Ed got you to sign that one contract while you were drunk?"

Fritz shuddered at the memory. *Plan Nine From Outer Space* would have killed his career if Ed hadn't agreed to use Bela instead. That near-disaster was enough to make him swear off alcohol forever.

He wished Jonquil would do the same.

※

About an hour later, the maid handed Fritz a package from the courier service. Half an hour after that, he was drunk enough to call Marty and beg him to find some way out of this deal.

"I don't understand," Marty said. "The show's titled *Star Trek*—what did you think it was about?"

"Sea captains used to navigate by the stars."

"What?"

"You said Roddenberry compared it to *Wagon Train*. Not all the settlers traveled by covered wagons. Some journeyed by ship."

Fritz leaned against the wall for support, waiting for Marty to respond.

"But it's a perfect part for you. There just aren't that many roles for science fiction types these days."

Fritz smashed his fist against the wall and a picture crashed to the floor. "I don't want to be a science fiction actor. I hate that stuff! Hate it! Hate it! Hate it!" He punctuated each word by pounding his fist against the wall.

"All right. Take it easy." Marty's voice was soft and soothing. "It's just one season. Go in and do your best. Get to know the folks in this business and maybe when this series dies, they'll offer you something you'll like a little better. I hear they're thinking about having a few detective series next season. Maybe I can line you up a pilot for one of those."

"Why can't you line it up now?"

"The studio doesn't work with people who don't follow orders."

Fritz sighed. "Am I stuck, Marty?"

There was a short pause, followed by, "Like a gnat on fly paper."

Fritz looked down at the glass on the table and said, "Okay. I'll be at the studio and I'll follow orders. But I want a good role after this. No more sci-fi. Okay?"

"You got it." Marty paused a moment, then added: "Just grab the money and run, Fritz. This series is too weird to last more than one season."

Fritz picked up the glass as he set down the phone. He stared at it for a moment, fighting for control. Which was stronger? His need to drink or his desire to become a great character actor?

He hurled the glass against the wall and turned around just in time to see the expression on the maid's face as she took off her apron and said, "I quit!"

❋

Fritz picked up the newspaper and spread it onto the floor, planning to scoop the glass onto it. A sheet of paper fell out and Fritz picked it up. He glanced at it; then reread it carefully.

David Gerrold? Who the hell was David Gerrold?

Fritz looked back down at the newspaper and remembered. The paperboy!

He found Jonquil in the kitchen, pouring another glass of wine. "You haven't paid the paperboy in nine weeks!"

Jonquil shrugged. "So?"

"He's holding our cat hostage until we pay him."

"Cat? Our cat's right here."

"Yes, but the neighbor's cat, Tribbles, is missing. I think this David Gerrold made a mistake and got the neighbors' cat."

She shrugged. "So let them worry about it."

Fritz started to say something, then paused. He took the bottle away from her and turned it upside down over the sink.

"The maid quit, and I'm not hiring another one. We're about to become very economically conservative. In fact, you're going to get a job. Would you like that, dear?" He stopped speaking and grinned madly at her.

Jonquil stared, her eyes widening as he threw the empty bottle into the nearest wastebasket.

"You're drunk!" she said.

"Yes. And for the last time, too. Both of us. We're going to dry out, and then I'm going to get you some kind of a job on the set so you'll stop spending the day imagining me flirting with cast members."

Jonquil swallowed hard before answering softly. "All right, dear. If it means that much to you."

He smiled. "And do you know what we're going to do with all this money we'll be making and saving?"

She shook her head.

"We're going to invest it in our own production company so I never have to take a role like this again."

❊

They both sat at the table the next morning, sipping their glasses of Alka-Seltzer and discussing the script lying between them.

"I can see why you got drunk after reading this," Jonquil said. "I wonder what the writer was drinking when he wrote it?"

"Poison, I hope," Fritz answered. "I would hate to think we're going to see more scripts like this."

"I think we should contact some of our old friends and persuade them to submit a few treatments to Roddenberry."

"Gene's not the problem," Fritz said. "It's the studio executives. I called Marty again last night, and he said they were convinced they'd lose advertising if crew members didn't smoke on the bridge."

"In a spaceship?" Jonquil shook her head. "Poor Gene."

She stared at the script on the table for a few minutes.

"I've got an idea. Why don't you call Joe?"

"Haldeman? Is he out of jail now?"

"He's been out for a several weeks. You don't serve that much time for burning your draft card. Besides, he got time off for good behavior."

Fritz laughed. "Yeah. I can see that. Turn Joe loose in a prison full of hardened criminals and in a week you'll have a bunch of laid-back hippies wandering around saying, 'Peace, brother.'"

Jonquil grinned. "Joe's just the kind of person you need to talk to those studio executives. "

Fritz shook his head. "One look at those love beads and granny glasses and the guards would throw him out."

Jonquil smiled and reached out for his hand. She squeezed it gently. "You call Joe and I'll take care of seeing to it that the studio executives listen to him."

Fritz squeezed her hand in response. "You don't need me to make the call. Do it yourself. I'll handle the crisis with the paperboy."

He was half-way out the door before she called out, "Where are you going?"

"To Ying's Chinese Brothel."

"What?"

"Relax. The newspaper boy works there part-time. He's a towel boy."

Jonquil arched one eyebrow. "Oh, really? Where does he—?"

"Don't ask," Fritz said with a wink.

Jonquil smiled and for a brief second he caught a glimpse of her the way she used to be, back in the days when they were both struggling writers.

"How do I know I can trust you?" Her voice was light and teasing, not the usual doom and gloom.

"I'll bring a note from the paperboy."

Fritz was rather surprised when he found the kid. He'd expected a little boy, not some handsome teenager.

"I came here to ransom the neighbor's cat," Fritz told him.

"Good. That will be eighty-three dollars."

"Eighty-three dollars? Nine weeks of newspaper delivery isn't that high."

"You need to cover the damages."

"Damages?"

David nodded. "The cat climbed up my mother's draperies while she was out and ripped them to shreds. Fortunately, Mom believed my story that the cat was a space alien."

"What?" Fritz shook his head, wondering if he'd heard correctly.

"I told her the cat mistook the draperies for a race of polyester beings who were determined to kill all carbon-based life forms by blocking their source of light and vitamin D."

"Your mother believed that?" Fritz stared at him, hoping the kid was joking.

David grinned. "Mom believes everything I tell her."

Fritz studied David for a few moments before being distracted by the sight of a young, scantily-clad Asian woman.

leading a handsome, well-known figure past them.

"Isn't that—?"

"Michael Resnick," David answered without any emotion in his voice. "He's a regular."

Fritz watched as they disappeared behind a door.

Another customer approached and stood beside the door with his eye to the keyhole.

Fritz turned his attention back to David. This kid had some weird ideas but at least he had an imagination. "Have you ever thought of trying your hand at writing sci-fi?"

David shook his head. "I'm working two jobs now to save money for law school. Why would I want to waste my time writing scripts?"

"It pays well."

David smiled. "Now that you mention it, I've always wanted to write sci-fi."

"Good. Tell me, what kind of story would you propose for a

series where a space crew is exploring the galaxy?"

"Do you have any kids in it?"

"Kids? Hell no. This is a spaceship, not a nursery school. No children on the bridge!"

"I think you're making a mistake there. You need a couple of teenage heartthrobs, too. That'll bring in the younger audience. Maybe you can get Annette Funicello and Frankie Avalon. Add a boy and his dog and you've got a real family program."

Fritz bit back an insulting remark and thought about this preposterous suggestion a moment. David might be on to something here. Some of the most popular and long-running programs, like Lassie, were those that appealed to kids. Maybe they could throw in a robot dog. Robbie would be a good name. Fritz rubbed his chin, considering the possibilities.

"Not a bad—"

His words were interrupted by the sound of gunfire. Fritz and David both dove to the floor as a young, naked Asian woman ran past them screaming, "Somebody call the cops! He's killed Michael Resnick!"

"That's it!" David stood up and extended a hand towards Fritz. "I just quit this job! How do I sign up for this script-writing position you mentioned?"

❄

David Gerrold's episode, *The Protracted Man*, was the first one aired and the show was an instant hit. The script Fritz hated was re-written by Joe Haldeman and titled *No More War*. It caught the entire nation's attention and led, indirectly, to a peaceful withdrawal from Vietnam.

Fritz found himself enjoying the role of Captain and the attention that went with it. Production companies which had snubbed him before suddenly started offering lucrative contracts for plum roles.

He and Jonquil celebrated the series's fifth anniversary quietly at home, with cake, ginger ale and some thick ledgers she'd managed to "borrow" from the accounting department.

❄

Fritz held Jonquil's hand as he blew out the candles on the cake. "Five years," he said. "Who would ever have believed it?"

Jonquil smiled. "Are we celebrating our years of sobriety or the anniversary of the series?"

Fritz grinned. "Yes."

Jonquil laughed and they kissed briefly before setting the cake aside and opening the ledgers.

"Now back to business," Fritz said. "Are you sure now's a good time to make a takeover bid on the studio?"

"Absolutely," Jonquil answered. "Gene's over-committed on those spin-off series. *Pioneer* is probably going to make it, but they're way over budget with the special effects. Now's the perfect time to make our move. I'm sure of it."

She closed the books and looked up at him. "So what will you do when you're in charge?"

He grinned. "Fire Billy Mumy. I'm getting tired of that kid saving the crew and I think the audience is a little sick of it, too."

"Careful, Fritz. He's pretty popular."

Fritz shrugged. "Okay, then we'll ship him off to the Academy. That way he can still make a few guest appearances but we won't be stuck with him every week."

Jonquil poured a glass of ginger ale. "And if you don't mind, I have some ideas for a line of toys we could bring out as a side business."

"Toys?"

She nodded. "I think little girls would love a doll to dress up in costumes, and Annette would make the perfect model for this. Action figures for the cast crew would be popular, too."

He choked back laughter as he saw the expression on her face. He shrugged. They could afford to lose a little money if it made her happy. "Sure. We'll fund a start-up company just as soon as the production company is in the black."

❊

Fritz tugged on his shirt as he stepped out onto the set. He liked the ninth season's jumpsuits much better than these things that kept riding up.

He grinned for the photographers as the camera crew wheeled the Tenth Anniversary cake onto the bridge and started cheering.

Jonquil stepped forward and kissed Fritz's cheek before handing him the traditional glass of ginger ale. "Happy anniversary."

43

He kissed her as photographers took their pictures.

"Thank you, everyone," he said. "I remember when no one thought the show would last a single season. Thanks in large part to Gene's efforts..." he paused and gestured in Gene's direction, "we're still here ten years later."

He looked around and raised his glass "To all of you. May the adventure never end." He hesitated a second. "But I'm afraid it's time for me to step aside so we can welcome a new captain. I'm no longer young, and the business of *Star Trek* has become overwhelming."

Jonquil grinned. He knew she was thinking of the toy business. That twelve-inch replica of Annette was the most popular doll in America and there wasn't a red-blooded American boy alive who didn't have a collection of *Star Trek* action figures.

Fritz looked out at the faces surrounding him. Even David Gerrold had stopped by for the party.

I wonder who's in charge at the governor's mansion. And is he really planning to make a bid for the presidency?

❀

Fritz leaned back in his recliner as Jonquil opened the door.

"Gene! What brings you here?" she asked.

He stepped inside and handed her a bottle of Ginger Ale. "How could I possibly miss your fifteenth anniversary? We really would have loved to see you two on the set today."

"Fritz is still recuperating from that accident on the ski slope with the Gerrolds."

"I would have been fine if his Secret Service agent hadn't bumped into me." Fritz said, struggling to stand up.

"What can I do for you?"

Gene took a deep breath and said, "I want to do another spin-off."

Jonquil arched an eyebrow and turned to look at Fritz.

"Isn't the schedule pretty full now?"

"Yeah, but somebody named 'Brin' has a great idea for a spinoff series with an uplifted dolphin named 'Darwin'. We're calling it *SpaceQuest*. There's an occasional part for an older, retired researcher and I thought Fritz might be interested in that."

Fritz grinned. "What's the uniform like?"

"A jumpsuit," Gene answered. "With a really neat patch."

"I'll think about it," Fritz said, looking at Jonquil.

She shook her head. "You'll take the part. You're just not happy unless you're acting." She smiled before adding, "I don't know how I could have ever thought you could be happy doing anything else."

Book editor, anthologist, best-selling novelist, and world-famous expert in vampire fiction, Greg Cox got his start in the working world as a phlebotomist, draining blood from winos for a living. Here he contributes a tale of another writer well-known for his preoccupation with oozing fluids.

—P.N.H.

GoH: H.P.L.
Greg Cox

Shortly after his eighty-fifth birthday, Howard Phillips Lovecraft slowly emerged from a taxi parked just outside the front entrance of the Sea-Tac Marriot. He squinted his eyes against the bright August sunlight. Where, he wondered, were all the clouds and rain he'd heard so much about? He glanced around his surroundings. An elevated sign mounted in the hotel parking lot read: WELCOME WEIRDCON '75!

Thank goodness they spelled "weird" right, he thought. So many people couldn't these days.

Although his aging bones ached from the taxi ride, and the long flight preceding it, he stood by chivalrously and held the door open as his wife carefully extracted herself from the cab's interior. "Are you quite all right, m'dear?" he asked her.

"Yes, thank you," Sonia replied cheerfully. Her doctor had suggested she forgo this long trip, given her recent health problems, but she refused to even consider it. She loved travelling. Indeed, he thought, she probably enjoyed these festivals even more than he did.

"Mr. Lovecraft!" a youthful voice called out. He looked up and found himself face-to-face with a skinny, hippie-ish, young man wearing a large rubber squid on his head. The tentacled thingie matched the cartoon Cthulhu decorating the name badge affixed to the long-haired youngster's tee-shirt. "I'm so glad you could make it. Let me help you with your bags."

Another weekend, another con. And in Seattle, no less! It was a long way, he thought, from Providence. . . .

❋

April 5, 1924
Hail, Belknapius!

Brace yourself, Sonny, for shocks greater than those that rattl'd Old
Pompeii. Thunderbolt after thunderbolt have struck the humble Lovecraft
household since my last missive winded its way to your door. Did I not, as
you well know, subscribe to an unshakeable conviction that the universe, in
all its cold & empty senselessness, cared not one whit about the meaningless
destinies of such insignificant creatures as ourselves, I might well believe that
Fate itself had conspir'd to disrupt the lives of this Old Gentleman & his
recently-acquired spouse, the estimable S.H.

Firstly, Henneberger attempt'd once more to thrust the editorial reins
of Weird Tales into my reluctant hands, upon the odious condition that I
establish lodgings in ugly, modern, crass, & repellent Chicago. Needless to
say, such an offer appalls more than it entices. Whilst the opportunity to
extend my own aesthetick throughout the good olde Tales has its temptations,
can you truly imagine that I, a venerable scion of stately New England, could
survive in such a vulgar, noisome metropolis? No, no, a thousand times no!
My roots extend into the dear, PreRevolutionary past, and my spirit requires
surroundings that bear the comforting weight of history & tradition. As
the Un-Dead Count says in Stoker's Dracula, "To live in a new house would
kill me." Indeed, and a new city even more so. Thus, I was fully prepar'd
to refuse our mutual publisher's beseeching offer once again.

And yet. . . .

Thunderbolt the Second: This may be hard for you to grasp, Belknapius,
but your Grandpa (in spirit, if not in flesh) is soon to become a father for
the first time. Yes, that's right. Your honourary Grandma, the former Sonia
H. Greene of the far-off Ukraine, informs me that the first of a new generation
of Lovecrafts is imminent. My gawd!

I must confess, the prospect is both daunting—and chastening. Were it
only for myself, the mere promise of steady employment, with its accompanying
financial security, would not be enough to lure me to the barbaric sweatshops
& stockyards of Chicago. Much would I prefer to live out my days in quiet
contemplation of the cosy lanes & somber cemeteries of my beloved Providence,
eking out the bare necessities of life with the meagre rewards afford'd me by
the fantastical scribblings of my pen. Alas, such a peaceful hermitage now
can never be.

I can no longer think only of myself. My duty to the Future outweighs *my longing for the Past. With a wife & family to provide for, I fear I must 'bite the bullet,' bestir myself from my accustomed haunts & habits, and accept the challenge of extracting sufficient quantities of filthy lucre to keep home & hearth together. No doubt the rough-and-tumble of the rat race will subtract years from my lifespan, but I see no other alternative.*

Do not be too surprised, therefore, if my next communication is postmarked "Chicago."

Yr. obt. ancestor,

H. P. L.

✳

After checking into his room and changing into a fresh suit, Lovecraft left Sonia napping and decided to check out the convention. A helpful fan pointed him towards the dealer's room.

Upon entering, he was happy to spy rows of tables covered with old books and magazines, many of them protectively wrapped in plastic. Even more gratifying was the lavish assortment of various Lovecraft products on display. He strolled down the aisles, automatically taking inventory.

There was the September issue, on sale just in time. He nodded approvingly; it was a good issue, with new stories by Lumley, Moorcock, and Ballard. Over there, on another table, was an impressive collection of back issues, several decades' worth. He spotted several more fans wearing squids on their heads, and dealers selling all manner of Cthulhu merchandise, from hats to buttons to the new line of Dunwich Horror action figures. *I'm probably not seeing a penny from half these items,* he sighed inwardly, but he hated to dampen the fans' enthusiasm by bringing up such annoying matters as copyrights; his agent often told him he was far too generous with the Mythos. Still, maybe he should have a lawyer look into these squids everywhere. . . .

On the other hand, after "Dreamquest II: Return to Kadath" opened this Christmas, he would have knicknacks enough to pay for his grandchildren's old age. The first film had turned Spielberg from an unknown director to a brand name, and increased Lovecraft's audience well beyond the college audience that had erected a cult phenomenon out of the Mythos and related works; the new movie was likely to be a merchandiser's bonanza.

A plump teenager whose name badge identified her as the

"Demon-Queen of Yrrrg" interrupted his business musings to ask him to sign a paperback copy of *Lovecraft's Universe of Fear #5: The Elder Gods at War.* As he scribbled his initials on the title page, she told him over and over about how much she had enjoyed it, and how it was the best thing he had ever written. He didn't have the heart to point out the small print on the cover that made it clear that this particular sequel was written by Bryan G. Stephenson.

But where was his own book? For a few minutes, while scanning each new table, he began to grow anxious. They had promised him the book would ship this week! Then, there it was, hot off the presses and piled up in stacks on the next table: *Cthulhu's Empire,* by H. P. Lovecraft, "New York Times Bestselling Author of *Cthulhu, Arise!*" He hefted the massive hardcover in his hands, admired the Frank Frazetta jacket with the embossed blood-red type. Good, he thought, they managed to get that rave *PW* quote onto the book at the last minute. Never mind what *Kirkus* said. . . .

Lovecraft smiled. At moments like this, he was glad that he had finally turned over the editorial chores on *Weird Tales* to young Steve King and gone back to writing.

✳

June 15, 1935
Dear Two-Gun,
　　My profound apologies for the inexcusable delay in answering your most recent letter. Three months, by Crom! It is a miracle that you did not send your bloodthirsty Cimmerian, gore-stained axe in hand, to avenge such desultory correspondence. I fear, however, that my editing chores at Weird Tales, *along with my own sporadic attempts at fiction, consume so much of my time that I must increasingly curb the amount of 'frivolous' (i.e. unrelated to* Weird *business) mailings I can indulge in. Funny, isn't it, that I, who once thought nothing of penning at least fifteen letters a day, would be reduced to such penurious economy & efficiency?*
　　(In fact, as a sop to my conscience & the Chicago work ethick, enclosed is the cheque for "People of the Black Circle." There!)
　　Still, I cannot complain overmuch. If placed upon a rack and tortured by the Inquisition, I would have to confess that I prefer editing to ghost-writing. Without too much false modesty, I am proud of our eerie little periodical these days, due in no small part to the fine efforts of you, Klarkashton, Bloch, & the rest of the gang. Chicago remains a ghastly abomination upon the

face of the Earth, and often I pine for the venerable shadows of Providence, but every day I am surprised to discover that I can endure what has to be endur'd, and that the challenge itself is curiously invigorating. S.H. & little Sarah appear to be thriving as well.

In fact, Bob, if I may presume so far, perhaps a sojourn beyond the boundaries of Bear Creek may have a salutary effect upon your own prospects. Without the spur of some jolt of reality, such as a major geographical translocation, we Dreamers in Darkness risk losing ourselves in our fancies & phantasies, letting our material lives & energies ebb away into some imaginative aether. (Not that your own barbarian energies show any sign of ebbing, by gawd!) And yet, I truly wonder if the harsh terrain of Texas is the proper dwelling-place for one of your poetical & historical sensibilities.

Hah! Listen to me lecture, like any doting Grandfather. You must indulge me. Inspir'd by my own example, I shall doubtless try to lure you all away from your native soil. The Homely Siren of the Windy City!

Well, back to work. No rest for the wicked or the Weird.

H. P. L.

❊

A heavy hand fell upon Lovecraft's shoulder, almost shaking the hardcover from his grasp, and a jovial voice boomed directly behind him. "Theobald, old siren! Welcome to the West Coast!"

Lovecraft recognized the voice instantly. "Two-Gun!" he said, turning around to face his old friend. Bob Howard, silver-haired and tanned, grasped his hand and gave it a firm shake. "I wasn't sure you were going to make it," Lovecraft said.

"Wild barbarians couldn't keep me away," Howard replied, "let alone Paramount or Universal."

Lovecraft rested his weight on the corner of the bookseller's table. "Speaking of which, how fares decadent Hollywood?"

"The usual. We're still trying to cast the new Conan TV show. The studio wants a 'name' like David Soul or Michael Landon, but meanwhile we're auditioning an endless stream of lifeguards and bodybuilders." Howard shrugged his large shoulders. "It's a dirty job, but someone has to do it. You know, some of these musclemen can barely speak English."

"To be honest," Lovecraft admitted, "I never really got used to Buster Crabbe as Conan."

"I know what you mean. Still, those old movies made my career,

50

not to mention all the westerns and Tarzan flicks I scripted back in the old days." Howard laughed. "And it's all your fault, for dragging my backside out of Texas."

"May the Gods of the Cinema forgive me!" Lovecraft said with mock horror.

"Hey, you have to admit that Ursula Andress made a great Valeria!"

✵

June 15, 1954

Notes From Arkham

Recently, a few of our most faithful readers have written in concern about an ominous, ongoing distortion they see at work in the pages of this venerable publication. They observe with alarm that, increasingly, good old-fashioned ghouls and graveyards are being supplanted by tales that draw on the revelations of modern science. Some correspondents even accuse us of abandoning the macabre for "that Buck Rogers stuff."

Well, yes and no.

Weird Tales *remains committed to prose and poetry that strives to imbue the reader with a sublime sense of fear and dread. True terror, however, is not confined to the cobweb-shrouded vaults of the Gothic past. In this Atomic Age, when the latest discoveries in physics unveil Reality itself as nothing more than an illusion composed of random probabilities, the most awe-inspiring horrors are those that brings us face to face with the immeasurable strange and terrible universe that science has exposed to our stricken senses. From the disturbing uncertainties of parallel dimensions to unnerving alien entities beyond our comprehension,* Weird Tales *will open your eyes, and chill your hearts, with the most transcendentally nightmarish vistas of today and tomorrow, as summoned into existence by such visionary imaginations as Philip K. Dick, Theodore Sturgeon, and Robert A. Heinlein.*

To our more traditional readers, let me assure you that vampires and hauntings will always have a home here, as well as masters of the uncanny like Matheson and Derleth, but your Doddering Editor sincerely believes that if this magazine turned away from the mysteries and wonders that lie ahead, contenting itself solely with the timeworn conventions of prior supernatural fiction, then our beloved Weird Tales *would not outlive the decade.*

A new era looms, in which we shall take take the best of science fiction,

51

fantasy, supernatural horror, and, yes, even poetry and "literature" to invent a new fiction of the fantastic so powerful and compelling that not even the dullest imaginations shall be able to extinguish or ignore us.

I hope all our readers, old and new, will join us in our eldritch odyssey into tomorrow!

❀

Lovecraft shivered behind the podium, whether from the air conditioning or emotion he was not sure. Dozens of fans and professionals had crammed into the large hotel conference room to hear him speak; it was standing room only and then some.

"You know," he began, speaking into the mike and gripping the podium with shaky hands, "I've thought of myself as an Old Man for so long—since I was twelve, probably—that it's a bit of a shock to attend an event like this, and to realize that now I really am old."

The audience, including Sonia, chuckled on cue.

"Some critics," he continued, thinking briefly of that damnable *Kirkus*, "maintain that I've lost my touch, that my new books lack the 'fear and power' of my earlier works." Lovecraft shrugged philosophically. "Who knows? Maybe they have a point. As I stand here basking in your greatly-appreciated warmth and support, and look back with gratitude on a long and interesting career, I suspect that my legendarily gloomy sensibility may have indeed lightened somewhat."

He paused to take a sip of water. Gazing out over the audience, he spotted Bob Howard, Sonia, the young woman with the autograph, and many more people he'd known and touched over the years. He felt a lump the size of Yog-Sogoth in his throat.

"I still believe," he said, "that the universe is essentially a cold, unplanned, and impersonal place, replete with enigmas we will never understand. But sometimes, at moments like this, I must admit that it doesn't seem quite so malevolent anymore."

Adorned with squids and smiles, the audience rose and gave him a standing ovation.

Louise Rowder sold her first four stories in 1994, and kept up the pace through 1995. This one is about the path an alternate Stephen King might have taken.

—M.R.

SIREN SONG
Louise Rowder

Stephen King stood in the doorway of his bedroom, an empty tube of toothpaste in his hand as he watched his favorite tie wriggle free of its hanger and slide under the bed. He sighed heavily as he crouched beside the bed and felt around for his tie. He found it and pulled. Something pulled back. A final yank and the ghostly hand released it.

"I thought you called an exorcist to get rid of this damned poltergeist," Stephen said to his wife. When he saw his wife's expression, he regretted the sharp edge frustration lent his words.

"I *did* call an exorcist." Her brows knit together over rapidly reddening eyes as she looked at him. Tabitha turned back to her makeup table and applied lipstick around her clenched teeth. "You were supposed to confirm the appointment. Anyway, I'm sure it's one of your relatives. None of mine ever had the bad manners to haunt the living."

Stephen wasn't sure what drove this reckless anger tonight. He knew his wife's danger signals. Maybe it was meeting this editor? Maybe it was having both his Hugos disappear off the mantle?

"No. *You* were going to set it up." Throwing caution to the wind, he continued, "And, if that weren't enough, we're all out of toothpaste." He punctuated the final statement by flourishing the empty tube.

Within a moment his wife stood before him. Swirling gray mist obscured her slender legs, red lights flashed in her eyes. She reached out with one clawed hand to tap him lightly on the chest. He fell back several steps, clutching the crumpled tie and toothpaste tube tightly in his hands. Tabitha moved forward, full of soft beauty and sharp menace.

"You knew I was a vampire when you married me! Of course I go through a lot of toothpaste!" She put her hands down and melted into a dark fog.

The vapor surrounded and lifted him out of the bedroom, berating him as it carried him down the hall. "Finish shaving and let me get dressed! It's hard enough dealing with two teenagers in the house. Always worried they'll show signs of the Change—that they're Recessives."

He shivered as she placed him gently back in the bathroom. A tendril of smoke placed another tube of toothpaste on the sink in front of him. His wife flowed back down the hallway, muttering about the idiocy of men in general and husbands in particular. The slam of the bedroom door cut off the rest of her words.

Shaking his head, he turned back to the mirror. Running the electric shaver over his chin and wondering what particularly unruly part of himself so wanted to provoke his wife.

Almost all the red in his beard had turned to gray. He felt an odd, jarring grief as he stared into his face. When had those lines deepened in his forehead? Maybe he should've stuck to the literary work he used to do—writing about the Recessives and their struggles in the ordinary world? Of course, that paid even less than science fiction. The family could barely scrape by now.

But he missed it sometimes—especially at times like this. He feared a meeting with another editor who would insist on splashing his novel cover with big-breasted aliens or weird organic spaceships. It didn't seem to matter that there weren't any spaceships in his stories, and there certainly weren't aliens with exaggerated glandular conditions.

He wandered into the living room, gathering up the notepad beside his favorite chair. One page fell free. Settling back in his corner chair, he began to daydream about hulking shapes in the sliding darkness . . .

A muffled call from the bedroom interrupted his reverie. Taking some of his scribbled notes with him, he tightened the belt of his bathrobe, and knocked softly on the bedroom door.

Tabitha opened the door with feline grace. She smiled a toothy grin and stretched invitingly in front of him, wrapping her long arms around his neck and pulling him closer.

"Well?"

"I'm sorry. I know I've been distracted lately. I'm just worried—" he started to explain.

54

"Shhh. Your Hugos will turn up and the dinner will be fine." Tabitha pulled some papers from his hand and smiled. "I'll always be able to find you—shedding papers like the cat sheds hairs."

Stephen enjoyed the cool feel of her flesh under his hands. "Are the kids with your mom?"

"Yes. You really are distracted today." She looked at him with concern, then licked the hollow of his throat and began working her way up his neck, nibbling gently. "I know the perfect way to relax you."

"Sorry, honey. But we *should* be getting dressed." Stephen glanced at the clock. He thought about putting on his suit for almost ten seconds before picking her up and carrying her to the bed. His papers falling free around them.

❋

"Your editor is a Grade-A Twit, and his wife! Wearing that garlic necklace! I wanted to strangle her with it," Tabitha said. She sat beside him in the car, wearing her wifely indignation like battle armor. "The advance was even lower than for your last book! And after winning two Hugos! What's the matter with those people?"

"I don't have much choice with the contract. You know that," Stephen replied, the words like broken glass in his throat. "Maybe I should go into a more artistic field, like Horror?"

"Give it some thought, dear." Tabitha understood his mood and reached across to lay a comforting hand on his knee.

Disappointment crouched in the darkness of the car—a heavy presence that weighted them into silence. The full moon reflecting off the wet highway seemed to guide them home. As they turned into the driveway the headlights illuminated a large animal. A swift blur of gray dashed across the lawn and disappeared into the hooded forest.

"Did you see that?" Stephen cried and pointed to where the large animal had disappeared.

"No. But I sure *felt* it." Her fingers trembled slightly as she squeezed his knee. "It's our son, Robert," she added in a hollow voice.

"How could he Change now? If he was going to Change, it should've happened at puberty."

His wife shrugged and opened the car door. Immediately she started to Change—her limbs melting to join with the moonlight.

A soft breath caressed his face. "I'll bring him home."

55

Stephen fumbled with the front door. It was almost unknown for Recessives to attack Normals. It was the *almost* that bothered him. He glanced back out into the yard and heard a distant howling. *Sounds like she got him,* he thought. Stephen hurried to check with his mother-in-law and find out what happened.

He reached for the phone but it was gone. Stephen demonstrated a gift for creative and convoluted profanities as he screamed imprecations at the poltergeist. After exhausting his supply of curses, heresies, and blasphemies, his imagination soared. When he finished saying "Obese, bug-eating blunderbison" a wrinkle appeared in the air.

A bright light slowly coalesced into a very rounded apparition wearing white shoes, a white belt, and a pale blue leisure suit.

"Uncle Vernon? I see death hasn't improved your taste in clothes," Stephen said with disgust. It wasn't that Tabitha was right about it being his relative but that she was right so often he found almost unbearable.

"I needed to talk to you," Uncle Vernon said in an echoey, nasal voice.

"I'm a pretty busy right now. Where's the phone? I need to call my mother-in-law."

"Your daughter's fine and your wife is bringing your son home now. You *heard* him howl. Tabitha isn't one to cross when she's mad."

"So why are you plaguing me? Where are my Hugos?" Stephen said, his face red with anger. He wished he had an etheric gun for pesky ghosts.

"I didn't take your Hugos," the ghost replied with an injured air. "I'm here to encourage you to stick with writing in the science fiction field."

Stephen simply looked at his uncle.

"Okay, I'm not exactly the most unbiased person in the world. I never much cared for the Recessives and the weird talents they have."

"Unbiased? You're still mad they eliminated the poll tax in Texas! You wanted to round up all the Recessives and stick them into camps!"

"At least I was catholic in my outlook. I thought everyone was inferior to me. But death has a way of moderating one's world view." Vernon glanced over at Stephen's desk. "I know things are tough in science fiction right now. But don't give it up for something as transitory as horror."

"If you wanted to tell me this, why not just write me a letter?"

"Hey, I haven't been dead *that* long. I'm still learning how to navigate. I discovered your anger gave me quite an etheric boost. I used it as a springboard to finally appear to you."

"I don't suppose you can tell me anything about the afterlife?"

"Of course not. Rules are rules," Vernon replied with reproach shading his voice.

"Well then, thanks Uncle. Guess this means goodbye. So long. Have a nice death," Stephen said cheerfully.

"I kind of like it here. Would you mind if I hung out a bit longer?"

Stephen shuddered. Then he remembered his uncle's weird taste in music. The man loved German operas and old crooners who sang songs with a slow and ponderous delivery.

"Sure. Stay as long as you like, but I've added to my CD collection." An evil grin lit Stephen's face as hit the play buttons on the stereo and cranked Charley Patton's "Rattlesnake Blues" up to full volume. "Not only Patton, but Rube Lacy, Muddy Waters, Howlin' Wolf. I'm going to play them all the time—full blast."

With a spine-tingling shriek, his uncle disappeared.

Rats! I forgot to ask him who took my Hugos, thought Stephen as he turned down the stereo.

A few moments later, his wife entered the house. She was holding their son by the scruff of his neck. He growled softly at her through the side of his mouth. She dropped him on the floor with a loud thump.

"Sit," Tabitha said, pointing at the couch.

Robert slunk over the couch; his tail tucked firmly between his legs. He circled about a few times before finally curling up. Resting his muzzle on his paws, he looked up at his parents with big soulful eyes.

"That look won't do you any good, young man. You've been Changing for a while. Don't even try to deny it. I don't know how I missed it. Your grandmother bespoke me while I was out hunting

57

you. She's certain it's been happening for months. No wonder you found so many excuses to avoid visiting with her." She turned to her husband. "Carrie will spend the night with my mother."

Stephen looked at his son with sorrow and a strange sort of pride. "Robert, there's nothing to be ashamed of. I don't understand why you hid it from us."

Robert slowly changed back into a naked sixteen-year-old, all arms and legs. A smattering of pimples across the bridge of his nose marred an otherwise handsome face. He had his mother's dark hair and exotic looks.

Stephen hid a smile as he watched his son color and cover himself with a seat cushion.

"You're always busy writing, Dad. If you're not writing, you're thinking about writing." Robert imitated his father's voice and tone. "I'm busy now. Don't bother me with it."

Husband and wife glanced at each other. *Didn't I tell you?* her eyes seemed to say.

"I'm sorry, son." Stephen thought about sitting beside his son but stopped when he saw how embarrassed Robert was. "Tabitha, could you bring Robert down his robe?"

Tabitha nodded and quickly left the room. She paused in the doorway to raise one eyebrow at her husband in silent command: Make this right.

A small suspicion crossed his mind. "Did you take my Hugos?"

Robert looked away and began vigorously scratching behind one ear with his hand in a sharp forward motion.

"Robert!" Stephen shouted, like a trumpet at Judgement Day.

"Yeah I took them." Defiance shone in his eyes, warring with anger and need.

"Where are they?" Stephen stood before his son, retreating again into anger out of habit.

"I tried to pawn them, but it wasn't worth it for the lousy five dollars the guy offered."

Stephen gasped. "Five dollars?"

"One of your Hugos is out in my tree house." Robert stared down at the rug. His knuckles whitened when he grasped the sofa cushion tighter.

"And the other?" Stephen was speaking slowly, remembering his high blood pressure. He was repeating the word: control, over and over in his mind.

"I was holding it when I changed. I . . . I'm not really sure. I think I buried it in the backyard." Robert drooped further into the couch as he spoke, as if seeking a den.

"*You did what?* Buried it!" Stephen's yells rattled the bookcases. He turned away from his son, feeling dizzy and strange. "Go upstairs; send your mother down."

Robert took one look at his father and sprinted for the stairs, screaming as he ran. "Mom! He's doing it again!"

Stephen fell to the floor, writhing briefly. Tusks sprouted from his mouth, warts covered his great shaggy body, and a bristly beard flowed past his waist. His suit lay in shredded rags around him on the floor.

"Can't you talk to our son without falling into ogre mode?" Tabitha tapped the floor with one slender foot.

Stephen grunted in reply.

"Well, let's go to bed. I sometimes wonder if every family has problems and arguments like we do," she said, tattered impatience in her tone.

Stephen bent his heavy head forward and followed her meekly up the stairs.

"You don't think his sister will change, too. Do you?" Tabitha asked anxiously.

Stephen prayed Carrie wouldn't.

❀

Dust motes danced in shafts of sunlight that came through the crooked windows of the tree house. Cobwebs filled the corners, water stains marred the walls, and some of the boards were loose or broken. It was a depressing, neglected place now. Stephen sat on the dusty floor feeling stiff and sore.

When had things gotten so complicated? Once, he could make his son laugh with delight by simply tossing him in the air.

Both Hugos sat on the floor. Stephen wiped a bit of dirt still clinging to one. Then he reread the note Robert had left for him. His son asked if Stephen still loved him, if he still cared. Was he really so neglectful toward his son? A tear rolled down his cheek to splash and blur the writing.

And yet . . .

Far away in his mind, he heard the whisper of dark things and laser blasts on alien soil . . .

Lyn Nichols broke into print in 1994, and sold ten stories in her first year as a pro writer. The fact that she feels neither gratitude nor loyalty toward Mike Resnick, who taught her everything she knows, will be apparent to you after reading this story.

—M.R.

KIDNAPPING KORIBA
by Lyn D. Nichols

The night was moonless and held the first hint of winter's bite. The old garage was a silent shadow, its open door a gaping maw. Above the door, a muted blue square marked the window of an apartment. In the distance, the kennel loomed large and dark, outlined by the security light on its far side. A dog barked twice, high and sharp, and another answered.

A white Lincoln Continental rolled to a stop beside the open door of the garage. A man stepped out of the car and looked around, the tip of his cigarette glowing red in the dark. Dropping the cigarette, he walked to the back of the Lincoln.

The man opened the trunk of the big white Lincoln and struggled to lift the blanket-wrapped bundle that lay within. It was heavier than it looked and awkward to handle, bending and twisting in his hands. He managed to lift half of the bundle out and let it hang over the lip of the trunk while he reached back in to lift the other half.

"Mffwl," the bundle said.

"Well, since you're awake, the least you can do is stand up," the man told it.

"Wrrmai?" the bundle said as the man heaved it the rest of the way out of the trunk, then: *"Urrrmmph!"* as one end hit the ground and wobbled.

The man steadied the bundle and collected his breath. Then, in a move remembered from younger, stronger days, he dropped his shoulder to the bundle's midsection and power-lifted.

"Oomph!" said the man.

"Ooof!" said the bundle.

The man shifted the weight on his shoulder and staggered into

61

the garage, trusting his memory to lead him through the dark to the door of the small storage room built into the corner. Halfway across the garage, his foot came down on something soft and yielding.

"*Yeow!*" he yelped as he and the bundle pitched forward into the dark.

"*Mrrow!*" the cat yowled.

"*Wmmmph!*" the bundle said as it hit the concrete floor.

The man climbed stiffly to his feet. "Sorry," he told the bundle as he rubbed a bruised elbow. He reached down to lift the bundle once more.

"Lemmelone," the bundle said, jerking away from his grasping hands.

The man stood and lit a cigarette, staring at the bundle. It thrashed around at his feet for a few seconds, then was still. A pitiful whimpering sound came from it. The man gave a disgusted sigh, knelt down beside the bundle, and untied the rope that bound the blanket. The blanket shuddered and a small, wizened face emerged.

"What . . . who . . . where am I?"

"Relax, Mr. Koriba. You're in no danger. You're going to be my guest for awhile." The man offered his hand. "My name is Mike Resnick."

"Have I been kidnapped?" Koriba asked rubbing his head. He ignored Mike's offered hand and struggling free of the blanket. "My family is not rich, we cannot pay a ransom. I believe you must have made a mistake, kidnapped the wrong man."

"Kidnapped is such a nasty, negative word," Mike answered, dropping his cigarette and grinding it under his toe. "Let's not call it that." He grasped Koriba's wrist and pulled him to his feet. "But there's no mistake, Mr. Koriba. You are James Edward Koriba of Kenya, aren't you?"

The old man nodded.

"You are an expert on Kikuyu and Maasai legends and folklore?"

The old man nodded again.

"Good. Then there's no mistake. This way, please." Mike led the old man to the storage room. He pushed open the door and reached inside to flip on the light.

A comfortable, cheery den greeted them. Cherry-wood bookcases lined two of the walls. Near the bookshelves, a matching pair of wing-backed chairs flanked a low end-table holding a delicate brass and glass lamp. A small bed with a blue comforter and throw pillows occupied one corner. At the foot of the bed, a cherry-wood dresser stood atop ornately carved legs. In the corner opposite from the bed was a colorfully painted privacy screen. Next to the screen a small refrigerator and low cabinet held a coffee-maker, a microwave and a hot-plate.

Mike pulled the little old man into the room. "Welcome to your new home, Mr. Koriba."

"I don't understand," Koriba said. "Why am I here?"

"We'll discuss that tomorrow," Mike said. "You're probably tired. Rest. Relax. There are snacks and soft drinks in the refrigerator. Good night, Mr. Koriba." Mike stepped out of the room and shut the door, turning the lock with a satisfying click.

James Koriba stood in the center of the small room and looked around. He scratched his head, confused. *Why did this Resnick man kidnap me?* he wondered. *What could he possibly want? And why does he provide such a comfortable cage?*

He crossed to the door and tested the handle. It was locked, of course; he'd heard the bolt sliding home.

Shaking his head, Koriba walked slowly toward the bed, his feet sinking deep in the plush carpeting. The clock on the dresser told him it was just past midnight.

The comforter looked warm and inviting, and the bed looked comfortable. He sat on it and bounced. A slow smile split his weathered face. The cozy accommodations suggested he was in no immediate danger, and Resnick had demurred at the use of the word 'kidnap,' preferring 'guest' instead.

I don't need to fear this man, he decided.

A yawn stretched Koriba's jaw. *And he was right about one thing,* Koriba thought. *I am tired.*

Koriba kicked off his shoes and wiggled his toes in the carpet. With a sigh and a shrug, he decided to wait until tomorrow to worry about this strange turn of events. Resnick had said he would explain things tomorrow.

He yawned again. *Tomorrow,* he thought as he discovered a

second light switch next to the bed. He removed his slacks and shirt, folded them neatly and placed them on the dresser. Slipping into the bed, he found it to be firm, comfortable, warm. Just right.

Tomorrow, he reassured himself once more as he flipped the switch and plunged the room into darkness.

❉

"Dad? Who's the man in the garage storeroom?"

Mike looked up from his book as Laura walked into the room. "Hi, Kid. What man?" he asked.

"The one that snored all night." Laura dropped to the floor next to her father's chair. "He kept me up half the night. I went to check this morning, but the door was locked."

"Oh. *That* man." Mike reached for his iced-coffee. "It's not important. Don't worry about it," he said, taking a drink. Laura grimaced as he chewed an icecube.

"But who is he?" she persisted. "If he's going to keep me up all night, I have a right to know."

Mike glared at his daughter. "Aren't you supposed to be back-packing across the Alps or something?"

"Who is he?"

Persistent brat, Mike thought. "He's a Kenyan folklorist," he said. "I kidnapped him. Don't tell your mother." He crunched down on another icecube.

Laura climbed to her feet. "Fine. Don't tell me," she said, starting for the door. "Just tell him not to snore so loudly." She paused at the door. "And no, not the Alps. My next trip will probably be to Italy."

Mike grimaced as she slammed the door behind her.

"What I want, Mr. Koriba, is stories. I want you to tell me all the tales and legends you know. Parables. Ngai and Gikuyu. I want ideas I can use as the basis for stories that I'll write. Stories I'll set in a science fiction universe."

Mike shook a cigarette from his pack and offered one to Koriba. Koriba declined.

"Please, Mr. Resnick—"

"Call me Mike," Mike interrupted as he lit the cigarette. "And don't ask me to let you go. You haven't told me any stories yet. When

I know the old legends of the Kikuyu, Maasai, Wakamba and other tribes of Kenya, then I will let you go."

"I was going to ask you to call me James," Koriba said with a shrug. "And there are a few things I'd like if I'm going to be here for awhile."

Mike raised an eyebrow. "Things? Such as?"

"A radio would be nice. It's terribly quiet in here. I'd like one with a cassette player, please." Koriba looked around the room. "And some tapes. Big band music, jazz, New Orleans or Chicago blues, torch songs."

"I'd also like some fresh fruits and vegetables. Pears, mangoes and bananas. Apples and oranges. Fresh broccoli, carrots, celery . . . just the usual assortment of snacks."

Mike grimaced. *Green stuff,* he thought. *Yuck!* "I stocked the cabinet with all sorts of good things to nibble on," he said. "Peanut butter, crackers, cookies."

"I don't eat peanut butter," Koriba said with a grimace that matched Mike's.

"Is there anything else you'd like?" Mike asked sarcastically as he walked toward the door.

Koriba smiled a small smile. "Yes. Could you ask the person upstairs not to make so much noise? He, or she, woke me several times this morning."

Mike almost choked. "I'll tell her," he managed to say. He stared at the door for a moment, then turned to face Koriba. "She commented on your snoring this morning. She said you kept her up last night."

James Koriba had the decency to look embarrassed. "Give her my apologies," he said. "I will strive not to keep her awake nights, if she will allow me to sleep through the mornings."

Mike nodded once and left. He didn't forget to lock the door behind him.

James Edward Koriba listened to Mike's footsteps recede. When he could no longer hear them, he leaned back in his wing-backed chair and laughed. He laughed until tears ran from his eyes and streaked his dark, withered cheeks.

Ah, Resnick, he thought. *You don't know the favor you have done*

65

for me! He glanced around the room. *I couldn't have found a better hiding place if I had tried. Tony Langoni will never find me here!*

Koriba chuckled, imagining the loan-shark's anger at finding—or rather, not finding—him at the card club on Tuesday. Koriba couldn't repay the ten thousand he'd gambled and lost, and had feared Langoni would break his leg, or worse. As long as he didn't give Resnick the stories he wanted so badly, he'd remain a guest. He'd be safe.

Koriba laughed again. *And Resnick wants those stories so badly he'll give me anything I ask for.*

❀

Mike was getting frustrated. Three weeks had passed since he'd borrowed (he wouldn't call it kidnapping; kidnapping is such an ugly word) Koriba. The Kenyan folklorist gladly answered any questions he asked, but instead of recounting legends, he gave dry dissertations of Kenyan history. Not even Mike's active imagination could pull usable material from them.

Not that they discussed the folklore that much. When Mike tried to direct conversation toward the Kikuyu god, Ngai, Koriba would somehow steer the conversation into discussion of one of Mike's books—a topic Mike found impossible to resist. Added to that, Koriba loved the horses, and often they would sit in the little den arguing the merits of the greats: Secretariat, Ruffian, Aladar, Man O' War. They also shared a love of Sondheim musicals, the Andrews Sisters, philosophy, collies, Teddy Roosevelt, and miniature golf.

Mike had lost count of the visits wasted in discussion of anything and everything except the Kenyan legends he wanted. And yet, he never felt other than completely satisfied when he left the old man.

Mike shook his head and reached for a cigarette. No, he never felt a visit had been wasted until he sat down in front of his computer and prepared to write. There were stories he could extrapolate from his own experiences in Africa, but none that grew from the wealth of lore he knew Koriba owned. He wanted that lore!

And at the end of every visit, the old man had a list of things he wanted or needed. Books. Cassette tapes. A television, VCR, and videos of the latest releases. Special meals. The man was costing him a fortune.

He had to get Koriba to give him something! He wanted to have a story—not just any story; he wanted an award-winner—to give to Ed Ferman at the WorldCon in London. And that was only two weeks away!

Mike decided that no matter what, he'd keep the discussion on Kenya when he went down to the garage this afternoon.

A few hours later Mike and Carol were going over some changes she insisted he needed to make on a manuscript. They were discussing the protagonist's motivation and whether he would have made the decision Mike had written or the path Carol suggested, when Laura knocked once and opened the door.

"Mom! Dad!" Their daughter bounced through the front-door waving a large envelope around. "I did it!"

"You did what?" Mike asked. "And quit jumping around, Kid. You're making me tired."

"What are you so excited about?" asked Carol.

"Oh, Mom! It's so cool. I've sold a story to *The Magazine of Fantasy and Science Fiction*. I can't believe it! Look!" She tossed the envelope on the table.

Carol fished the paper out and unfolded it. A proud smile lit her face as she read. "Oh, Laura. This is wonderful!" She held the paper out to Mike.

Mike glanced at it. He scanned the important lines; he was familiar enough with Ferman's contracts. "Not bad, Kid," he said. "What's this story about? And where did you get the title, *Kirinyaga*? Doesn't that mean something like 'bright mountain' in Swahili?"

"No, Dad. It means 'mountain of light' in Maa, the Maasai language." Laura said. "And that's the weird part. I've been having these really bizarre dreams. Almost like someone is telling me these really neat stories about a Kikuyu tribe in Kenya. I just waffled them around a little, set them up on a Utopian planet in the far future and centered them around a *mundumugu*—a medicine-man—named Koriba."

Carol stood up and hugged her daughter. "Isn't it wonderful, Mike? Laura's following in your footsteps."

Mike smiled, albeit a bit stiffly. "That's great, Kid. *F&SF* isn't an easy market to break on a first try."

My stories! he raged inwardly. *Somehow, Laura has been getting the legends Koriba hasn't been telling me. But how?*

"I've got to go back to my apartment and write some more," Laura was saying. "I'm working on one now that I'm calling *The Manamouki.* It's a Swahili word. Did you know you can't say woman in Swahili? *Manamouki* is the closest you can get. It means female, but means more like female property. It's used to describe cows, bitches, ewes, sows, as well as women.

"I've still got several more of these Koriba stories to write after this one's done." She grinned. "I need to get them all down on paper. I'm terrified I'll forget them, or that the dreams will stop!"

She kissed Mike on the cheek and hugged Carol before dashing out the door.

❊

Mike knocked on the store-room door and waited for Koriba's acknowledgment before unlocking it and walking in. He didn't bother to shut the door behind him; it didn't need locking any longer.

"You can leave any time you want," he said to Koriba.

Koriba looked up from the chair where he sat reading. "You've all the information you need for your stories?" he asked.

Mike shook his head. "I've decided to write about Egypt instead. I've got this wonderful idea for a story I'll call *Death on the Nile.* It's a sure winner. Besides, Africa's been done already."

Koriba looked around the room that had become his home. A distant—almost melancholy—look crossed his face.

"Do I *have* to go?" he asked.

Mike stared at the old Kenyan. "You don't want to leave?" Koriba shook his head and looked at Mike. Mike swore there were tears in the little man's eyes. "I don't get it," Mike said. "I kidnapped you. You're supposed to hate me. I should be worried that you'll go running to the police to have me arrested."

"Let's not use the word 'kidnapped,'" Koriba said, shaking his head. "It's such an ugly, uncivilized word. I'd much prefer to consider myself your friend and guest." He shut the book and set it on the table beside the chair. "Listen, Mike. I've enjoyed our conversations. I've enjoyed my stay. I'd like to remain longer if you'll allow it."

"Why?" Mike asked.

"Because I haven't been straight with you," Koriba admitted. "I haven't been telling you the legends you wanted to hear."

Mike crossed to the second chair and sank into it. "I *knew* it!" he said to himself. "I knew you were stalling me!"

"Yes. I didn't want to give you the tales, because I didn't want you to let me go." He looked Mike directly in the eye. "I've been hiding from a loan-shark who'll probably kill me if he finds me. I owe him ten grand."

Mike shook his head. "I don't get it," he said. "You weren't telling me the legends, and my daughter the romance writer just sold a Kikuyu story about a witch-doctor named Koriba. It doesn't make any sense."

Koriba's head jerked. "Your daughter? Is she the young lady that lives upstairs?"

Mike nodded. "Laura."

"Uh-oh." Koriba buried his face in his hands. "It's my fault," he mumbled.

"What do you mean, it's your fault?" Mike asked. "Has she been speaking with you?"

"No." Koriba stared at the ceiling. "I didn't want to keep her awake with my snoring," he said softly. "To keep myself awake I've been reciting legends and parables, practicing the cadence and flow of the tales." He shook his head and sighed. "She must have heard me."

Mike stared at the carpet as he thought about the entire chain of events. Suddenly he laughed. "She'll probably win a Hugo with that damned story," he told Koriba, chuckling. "Hell, she'll probably win a Campbell, too."

"Ngai is a wise god, Mike," Koriba said. "There is always a reason for the things that occur."

"So you've told me. Any idea why all of this has happened?"

"Nope," Koriba said, shrugging. "I'm not a *mundumugu*. I just tell stories about them." Suddenly he grinned. "But I'll bet fifty dollars against another week of hospitality that I can come up with a parable that will fit."

Madeleine Robins is the author of several SF stories published in the last few years, several Regency novels published well over a decade ago, and a novel currently in progress for Tor Books. She is a graduate of the Clarion Writers' Workshop. Here she gives us behind-the-scenes look at that legendary institution, and at the brilliant husband-and-wife writer team that has guided it from its inception.

—P.N.H.

SIX WEEKS, NO EXIT
Madeleine E. Robins

It's hard to explain what we wanted—in some mysterious way we were there, all of us, to become more meaningful. To experience life, unconstrained by our usual habits and surroundings, our jobs, our spouses, our weight- and drug- and drinking-problems. I was Ginnie, then. From Hauppauge, New York, with a BA in English literature and a longing deep in my soul to bare my inner truth, bare it lyrically. At the time, of course, I thought I merely wanted to be able to sell to *Asimov's*. The program's administrators did not disillusion me. Soon enough I, we all, would learn the true meaning of Clarion.

Enough has been written about Clarion: how the program works, its history. For the first four weeks the workshop is taught by American luminaries such as Bryant, Ellison, Butler, Carr—the list is, by now, almost legendary. The last two weeks, of course, are always taught by Clarion's founders, Jean-Paul Sartre and Simone de Beauvoir. For me, for most of the class, the first four weeks were only the preamble to our meeting with the true masters.

I barely remember the first week. It may have been the whirl of activity, or the late hours, or the tequila. On the whole I rather think it was the tequila. The first morning we sat waiting for an instructor who never appeared, until it dawned on us that this was our first lesson in the essential futility of art. So we invented ourselves, or at least our workshop, reading each other's stories, ripping them to pieces with truly professional vitriol, reducing each other's egos to sodden pulp, anesthetizing it all with Dos Equis. In the cheap pile of the hall carpets you could trace the progress of the love affairs to

70

which our painful emptiness drove us: from this bed to that, to another, footprints progressed with deliberate abandon. It was the writer's life as I had always believed it must be.

Still, satisfying as our new lives as writers were, all of us knew that the last two weeks of the program would bring the true transformation. Even before the arrival of Sartre and de Beauvoir their presence could be felt. By the end of the first week we were all smoking Gitanes—all except for Frank from New Mexico, who had changed his name to François and was smoking Gauloise. Often he and I would sit up late in a haze of blue smoke, nestling among the empties and talking of truth and writers' markets.

The second week brought Harlan Ellison: we'd heard the stories, of course. They were all true. He strode the earth like a giant—well, perhaps not a giant. Each morning he would line us all against the wall, then storm up and down, pointing impatiently to one, then another. "You: when's the last time you changed that T-shirt? You: nuke the corduroys, for Christ's sake. You: you dress like a bimbo: you wanna be an artist? See me after class. Ah, hell, I need more coffee," he would finish, and stalk out.

To the void left by his retreating form François asked—but quietly— "Does it matter what one wears—angora or twill? I mean, what does it matter?" I nearly loved him then; in fact, I did, later that afternoon.

Connie Willis had a passion for detail, detail, detail. "A little more blood in the scene with the axe would be nice," she said mildly. Or "I think maybe you need a dead dog in the corner, to give it a little character. That's just a suggestion, of course. What do you think?" Driven from the workshop each afternoon by her relentless emphasis on nuance, we abandoned ourselves further to empty bacchanalia. Willis refused to participate—or rather, did not so much refuse as sit and watch us each evening, occasionally murmuring "Golly!" as our lives churned on around her.

Then came Budrys, the prelude to our true encounter. I don't know what we expected, but he was nothing like it: a monument of a man looking over the rim of his coffee cup at all of us with an air of truly existential ennui. The first morning he sank into his chair like a man settling himself for a profound seige, and looked around at us all.

"Okay, enough of the crap," Budrys sighed. "I'm here to talk about plot. You take a violin, you take a golden haired moppet. Throw in a little jeopardy, up the stakes, add the validation. Any questions?'

François raised his hand. "What about truth?" He cocked an eyebrow and sneered.

Budrys shifted in his chair and fanned the air like a God swatting at a gnat. "Oy. Look: you get a violin, a moppet, up the stakes. Truth will follow. Do you get what I'm saying to you?"

François refused to be cowed. "What about meaning?" he asked. He was beautiful in his rebellion; his shabby black beret drooped over one eye, the Gauloise dangled from his lower lip.

"What about setting?" Budrys countered. "And characterization. And pacing. Style. Humor. Theme." The bullying was merciless, and it went on and on, as Budrys talked about syntax and dramatic structure and internal coherence.

That afternoon many of us gathered around François as he wept, unashamed, sitting in front of his room. "It doesn't matter," he said at last. "When Sartre comes, *he'll* understand."

That week was the hardest, not just on François but on all of us. On Friday someone found a store mannequin of a child, spray-painted the head gold, and brought it in to burn in effigy; but by that time no one had the heart for such rebellion, and the golden-haired moppet simply took its place in the classroom with the rest of us. Budrys, except for a pause as he drank his morning coffee, never seemed to notice the addition.

At last, on a rainy Sunday evening when the dining hall was closed and there was nowhere to get coffee, they arrived. The whole class was there to greet them, sitting expectantly in the dark while they opened the door and fumbled for the light switch. To yell "surprise!" would have been gauche, we knew. So in the end we simply sat there and watched as de Beauvoir and Sartre lugged their sodden suitcases into the room.

De Beauvoir turned and regarded us. "Merde," she said succinctly.

"Oui," Sartre agreed, and headed for the bathroom.

A few vital images stand out from those two weeks: Sartre

entering the class the first morning with a hand full of superballs; casting them wildly into the room and watching as we ducked and hid behind raised hands. Once the balls had come to a rest, "You see that something, once set in motion, becomes unpredictable, random?" he asked. We nodded as one. "What I mean to say is, who cares?"

While Jean-Paul always watched our waterfights, applauding each time a girl in a T-shirt got drenched (once he even joined in, dropping a bucket of sand on François's head by mistake), de Beauvoir seemed to spend all of her time making notes. Each morning she would appear for the workshop, smoking and drinking coffee, inscrutable in a mannish suit, her hair in its chignon the essence of Parisian chic, just thirty years too late. In each critique, when her turn came, she would draw deeply on her cigarette, look sidelong at Sartre, then, as if reading something there which was not visible to the rest of us, say in her throaty voice, "Pass." And in that word we heard experience of ennui driven down the corridor of years at gale force.

From the first we all wanted to please our mentors, but none so much as François. He abandoned my bed and lived on Doritos and instant coffee, composing a story a night, each more cunningly obscure, each more searingly truthful. But somehow they missed the mark. Each morning Sartre would demonstrate with ruthless elegance the essential lack of futility in François's latest fable. Each morning de Beauvoir would drag deeply on her cigarette and say "Pass."

Not that the cooling of François's ardor troubled me: I understood what he was striving for. But without him to occupy me, my nights were curiously empty. Empty, that is, until the evening when Sartre asked me to meet with him privately to discuss my work. In a seventh heaven of bliss which I realized only later belied the spirit of existential angst, I met him in an empty classroom. I sat and listened as he talked of the bleak void that my work encompassed, and knew even then that he thought I had that special spark he sought. Finally matters came to a climax.

"Merde!" he said harshly, and crushed me to his breast. "I must have you!"

"Jean-Paul, this is so sudden," I said. "What about my stories? And anyway, I thought that you once said you preferred croissants to sex."

"It was brioche." Behind the thick lenses of his glasses Sartre's eyes were incrutable. "And we are in East Lansing, Michigan. There are no croissants. Come here."

I gave myself up like a moth to the candle, and called it destiny.

❋

What extraordinary days those were! My pleasure was marred only by the spectacle of François, who was making himself pathetic by trying to ingratiate himself with de Beauvoir. It was embarrassing; when at last de Beauvoir took pity on François and took him as her lover, the rest of us could only shake our heads at the banality of it all.

On the last morning of the workshop, François had submitted one last story for critique. What could any of us say to him? It was rife with detail, plot, setting, characters. The style was engaging, the voice knowing yet compassionate. In it there was not one true moment of ennui or angst. What had happened to the François with whom I had spoken burningly of the bleak void of writers' markets? In my pity I compromised myself, pursed my lips and said "tres interesante," before deferring to the next critic. It was Sartre, at last, who broke the spell.

"Merde," he said coldly. "Tripe. This story is unshaped, it has no essence. You have not revealed yourself."

François sat dumbly, glancing de Beauvoir . She examined the cuff of her tweed jacket coldly; there was no help for him from her.

"Anything else?" François asked at last, low.

Sartre shrugged. "Your prose is meaningless. Also, I'm sleeping with your girlfriend," he added laconically, and drew upon his pipe.

There was silence in the room. All eyes went to de Beauvoir. After an eternity of silence she said "Pass." She smiled a smile of perfect complicity at Sartre.

In a moment François had jumped out of his seat. "You bastard, I'll kill you!" François shrieked, and jumped on Jean-Paul, clubbing him with the arm of the golden-haired moppet, which had unaccountably come detached. Simone sat there, entranced, the smoke from her Gitane curling slowly to the ceiling. After five or six blows we managed to pull François away from Sartre. Jean-Paul straightened up in his chair, took his hands down from around his head, and puffed thoughtfully on his pipe.

"Are you all right?" Simone asked at last.

"How can it possibly matter?" Jean-Paul said. But he took her hand and they exchanged a look of such exquisite understanding and ennui that I understood, at last truly understood, that I would never be more to him than a momentary abberation. In that moment's pain I began to grow up.

It is fifteen years later. Most of us scattered to the four winds. A few of us continued to write. François changed his name back to Frank, and went to work as a columnist for *Esquire*, where he has won several prizes. I returned to Long Island, living in my parents' basement and working by day at a series of meaningless jobs in the fast food industry; by night I wrote, as I do to this day. You hold the fruits of that long fifteen years' labor in your hand. All that I know of truth and of ennui I have put in this book; I only hope that you can feel it as I have done.

And so, this book is for Jean-Paul and Simone, who made my heart break so that I could make the book sing.

Leah Zeldes is a long-time fan, a Hugo-nominated fanzine editor, and a professional writer. For this story, she chose to write about a handful of skiffy writers living in Paris in the 1920s.

—M.R.

HEMINGWAY, REMARKS ARE NOT LITERATURE

From The Autobiography of Alice Z. Toklas

by Leah A. Zeldes

A rocket is a rocket is a rocket is a rocket, said Gertrude Stein. This was in Paris at the atelier at 27 rue de Fleurus. There was a great excitement at her words. Exactly, Hemingway said.

He had published The Sun Also Rises about a planet with such an erratic orbit that the sun only set subjecting the inhabitants to nightfall once every thousand years and quite a number of astronomers had found fault with its science. He was very discouraged by this at first but later found the controversy between the scientists and the literary people created a lot of notice of the book.

Gertrude Stein said H.G. Wells did not go into a lot of details about his Time Machine nor Jules Verne about his underwater device, the vision not the nuts and bolts are the core of the work. She has a great passion for exactitude but it must be done so that it is perfectly clear, if it cannot be clear it is better left out, she insists.

Gertrude Stein has a great feeling for H.G. Wells even though she has never met him. They were always going to meet but somehow it never happened. But he wrote her a very enthusiastic note in connection with her first book and it meant so much to her.

It was about this time that Hugo Gernsback began Amazing Stories. Gertrude Stein was afraid that it would be too nuts and bolts. There are no publishers in America who like adventure, she said. She sent Amazing some manuscripts, not with any hope of their accepting them, but if by any miracle they should, she would be pleased.

Amazing used a great many reprints from H.G. Wells and Jules Verne and Edgar Allan Poe so nuts and bolts were not the problem.

I do not know what the difficulty was, but Gertrude Stein received a long letter saying her materials were not without interest but that of course Amazing readers could not be affronted by them. Gertrude Stein was delighted when later she was told that Gernsback had said in New York that the work of Gertrude Stein was very fine but not for us. Later of course they did print Elucidation, the novelette If He Thinks, and As A Wife Has A Cow, A Love Story with beautiful illustrations by Juan Gris. By then Elliot Paul was editor, but of that later.

To come back to the events that were happening.

Fitzgerald naturally did not agree with Hemingway and Gertrude Stein although This Side of Paradise is very vague on the details of the future world where it takes place. Fitzgerald is more interested in people than landscape. Gertrude Stein says this book really created a new alien culture. She has never changed her opinion about this though Fitzgerald now admits he used Africa as a model.

Gertrude Stein and Fitzgerald are very peculiar in their relation to each other and often disagree. Gertrude Stein said that Fitzgerald was the only one of the younger writers who wrote naturally about people. She says it is equally true of The Great Gatsby, Fitzgerald's book about the man who sold the moon. Fitzgerald always says that Gertrude Stein says these things just to annoy him when he is trying to make a point in the other direction and it is very cruel. They always however have a very good time when they meet.

The last time they had a very good time with themselves and D.H. Lawrence. Gertrude Stein likes Lawrence, though she did not admire The Lost Girl. She said the story of a fat young girl on Mars was dull and commonplace. Mars is too exotic a locality for such a flat character, Gertrude Stein feels. She prefers a more lyrical approach, such as Upton Sinclair's view of Venus in The Jungle. Gertrude Stein is a master of the commonplace, but she says it is no use pretending that a place like Venus or Mars can be common.

Hemingway disagreed about this. They also disagreed about Virginia Woolf and Willa Cather. Hemingway said Gertrude Stein herself was the only woman writer who really understood the scientific fantasy. Gertrude Stein was very flattered and touched but said that was absurd. After all look at Mary Shelley, she said.

Hemingway did not find Cather's People and their psi powers very likely. He thought Cather too allegorical.

Likelihood has nothing to do with allegory, said Gertrude Stein. She said One of Ours and A Lost Lady provide wonderful portraits of the way aliens in our society represent emblems of our better selves and if that was allegorical it still was stimulating and realistic. And as for Woolf, she is very likely, The Voyage Out is just what Gertrude Stein thinks emigration to a new space colony would be.

I always used to say that Hemingway was a misogynist and when Men Without Women, his story of a single sexed race, came out I felt quite vindicated. However, whatever I say, Gertrude Stein always says, yes I know but I have a weakness for Hemingway.

Gertrude Stein contended there were plenty of great women writers in the field. She pointed also to Edith Wharton whose time travel story The Age of Innocence won the Pulitzer Prize.

Hemingway argued that Edith wrote utopian literature not scientific fantasy. He said her books had not enough science in them.

We are back to nuts and bolts again, said Gertrude Stein.

The editorship of Astounding *clearly exerts a fascination in Alt-Skiff studies (as we buffs call it) comparable to that surrounding the Civil War in mainstream alternate-history research. Ever equal to scholarly challenges, SF writer and critic Gregory Feeley channels an outrageously plausible continuum in which the great Street and Smith magazine was guided by an entirely different hand.*

—P.N.H.

SCATCHOPHILY
Gregory Feeley

> He developed a sudden, intense interest in Colorado, because the sound of the name conjured up visions of majesty and romance. Denver and the Grand Canyon struck him as particularly appropriate for a long rhythmic poem, and he began to daydream about going there.
>
> —Deirdre Bair, *Samuel Beckett*

> The allwhite poors guardiant, pulpably of balltossic stummung, was literally astundished over the painful sake.
>
> —*Finnegans Wake*

The sun glittered on the pier-slapping waves, rising just over the harbor, as happened in Dublin (when there was sun) but never Le Havre. Beckett looked past the Statue of Liberty, where he had expected to be admitted to the New World, to the scattered ships on the horizon, wondering which was the *Champlain*. It did not seem an especially auspicious name for the ship that was carrying the great man to Armorica.

Beckett looked without impatience at his watch, which noted that opening time lay yet three hours away. Foolish to expect liners to keep to a timetable like trains, yet the wireless had announced the ship's arrival by ten this morning. Already a man who looked disreputably like a reporter was lurking near the quay.

He shifted the mass under his arm, an inky batch of proofs that would have to be finished this afternoon. A lovely land, America, where you could come in to work late so long as you took your labors home at night. He sometimes marvelled that he had not yet left

79

behind a bale of manuscript, like Murphy's ashes, to be trampled into the spume beneath the stools of some Manhattan bar.

It occurred to him that the solution to his chores might lie to hand. Four Futurians, scrubbed red as lobsters in ill-fitting suits, stood at the railing, looking to sea with mingled expressions of deferential awe and defensive disdain. Had they not come round at seven he would yet be abed, a service for which he must finally be grateful.

Still, he would not scruple to put the lads in harness. Unrolling the proofs, Beckett checked their number and divided by five, which produced a gratifyingly modest quotient. Amazing that the ancients took so little consolation in mathematics.

"It's an hour to docking, and I've scribbles to muck through. You boyos willing to lend a hand?"

Pohl, who was editing two rags of his own, looked dubious, but the rest seemed game. "These are *Unknown* proofs?" one of them asked.

"Aye, lad, not a rivet in the lot." Though he saw looks of misgiving in even the college boy, Beckett made no secret of his preference for the newer magazine. Little of what he published was astounding but much would remain unknown.

They settled about one of the picnic tables provided for the apparent purpose of allowing New Yorkers to share their lunches with the gulls, and Beckett handed round the long galleys. These tended to scroll back up or flap in the wind, but Kornbluth produced from his pocket a collection of smooth stones, presumably gathered in order to be skipped across the waves. Beckett fingered one absently. Flanneltongued after a long night's indulgence, he felt the strange urge to pop it into his mouth.

The reporter evidently recognized the long galleys spread on the table, for he started toward them with a brisk step. As he neared, Beckett recognized him as a fellow Irishman, albeit one got up as a rich Yank.

"This looks like the offices of *The Little Review,*" he remarked in a brash American accent. The four Futurians looked up.

"Do we look like old ladies?" asked Blish nastily.

"Sorry." He offered a bad-boy grin that made Beckett stiffen. "I'm from the *New Yorker*, and I'm here to cover Mr. Joyce's arrival in America. And I know a tableful of magazine editors when I see one." He was trying to read the running title on the nearest galley.

"You're looking at the next issue of *Unknown*," said Lowndes stoutly. "It is a magazine of fantasy and science fiction, the literature of the future, and James Joyce is the world's greatest fantasy writer." Beckett winced.

"Is he, now?" The reporter seemed amused.

"You bet." It was Blish, quick to detect condescension. "Joyce's two great novels include werewolves and ghosts, fairies and giants. They are great fantasies, that encompass all of fantasy and literature before them."

"That's fascinating." The reporter, who was younger even than Beckett, had sized him up as this crew's apparent leader. "And are you waiting to meet Mr. Joyce in the hope of recruiting him as a contributor?"

Beckett flushed and said nothing. To his horror young Kornbluth spoke up beside him: "Mr. Beckett has known James Joyce for over ten years, and will certainly be publishing him in the New World."

"Mr. Beckett?" the reporter asked, studying him more closely. "Are you perhaps Irish?"

✳

Gulls screamed and dove for bobbing pieces of thrown bread, profane burlesques of the Paraclete. The White Russian, who had proven informative on matters of Slavic taxonomy but had otherwise not held his interest, was standing beside Joyce as Lady Liberty rose torch first from the sea, like Venus in search of an honest man.

"Now would she be the mother of Uncle Sam, then?" Joyce inquired, returning to the mythological theme he had toyed with throughout the voyage.

"I don't believe so," the White replied. "In Russian, the Devil has a grandmother but no other relative. I suspect our new uncle stands similarly bereft."

"O, that cannot be. Grendel has his dam, and even Gog his Ma. John Bull has a mother, you may be sure."

"I believe that Uncle Sam preceded Lady Liberty," said the Russian politely, "who was given to the Americans by the French."

"Which is only appropriate, as France gave birth to the United

States," said Joyce properly. "And it is the *Champlain* that bears us to North America, which Champlain named Nouvelle France." The ship's name pleased him, though he had been sorry to learn that it was not of the Cunard line. "Ladies of the Cunard line have frequently promised me assistance," he had told Nora, "and I had hoped their promises were to be redeemed at last."

"And what would *her* name be?" the Russian asked.

"Eh?"

"The mother of John Bull. Boadecea, perhaps? Elizabeth?"

"Emma." Joyce said it firmly. "Stolid British name, redolent of soap-reddened hands. Misses Austen and Brontë each had her *Emma*, and so have most of their bluestocking successors. It is the quintessence of British womanhood, flat and unmusical, a dying trochee."

"Not so mellifluous as Molly," the White observed. Joyce glanced sidelong at him. He had gathered that the fellow was a literary figure in the emigré world, and that he was familiar with Joyce's work and evidently didn't care for it.

"Indeed no, or Anna Livia. Perhaps my next heroine, a shipcaptain's daughter and an American, will bear a homely British name, but I doubt it."

"You have a new work in progress?" the emigre inquired politely. Joyce could not quite hear italics.

"It is being carried *in utero* to the new world, as perhaps my heroine shall be," he said, struck by the happy thought. "I could well write of America and its filial revolt from withered England, America and its poor cousin Ireland, America and the Negro. *Lavnegro*. Are there gypsies in America?"

"I don't think so," the Russian replied. "There are Indians, though."

"Pocahontas died in chill England," Joyce mused. "And Benedict Arnold."

"America is also a land of prizes; every tycoon has an award or university chair named after him." The Russian inclined his head toward the Manhattan skyline, now rising on the horizon. "Perhaps they will give you one."

"The Prix Joycean?" asked Joyce, misunderstanding slightly. "Too late for that; I am prix fixe, my standard suitable for no foreign currency. Should anyone suggest otherwise, they will be disabused *poste joyceanne.*"

The sun, rising over the ship, broke through the opening between its stacks to fall upon the patch of deck the two men shared. Joyce, who could not see either statue or buildings, felt the warmth spill over him and smiled. Somewhere ahead of them, a harbor tug lowed.

"Abeam, alight," he cried softly. "At noon over Greenwich, yet still dawning over the vinelands, the newenglands and -frances that old empires sowed and lost. While old Europe tears at itself we are borne west, kohls to new kessel, across the Atlantic's *champ laineux* to my New Found Land."

❀

By the time the *Champlain* had eased into its berth, a considerable crowd had collected along the quay. Most seemed to be relatives, anxious to see their loved ones safely out of Europe, but Beckett could see a number of photographers, accompanied by reporters with Press signs in their hatbands. They seemed to be from the local newspapers, and looked considerably scruffier than the smooth-talking Yalie still beside him.

"So you wanted to see the Wild West, but got no farther than Manhattan?" The reporter sounded casual, as though merely chatting.

Beckett could see the beginning of a Talk of the Town piece, which was this fellow's beat if anything was. "Ran out of funds getting this far. Even passage on a tramp steamer comes dear in Irish dollars."

"You came in one of those tubs?" the reporter asked, as though incredulous. He was evidently facile in drawing folks out.

"Your namesake crossed to America in a coracle," Beckett observed.

"And you got a job editing pulp magazines," the reporter marveled.

"The position was open," Beckett said shortly. Four books, none of them published here nor likely to have impressed Fred Tremaine had he asked to see them. Beckett had won the job over one of the magazine's regular contributors, possibly because Fred was already contemplating launching *Unknown* and imagined that a magazine devoted to tales of bogles and wee folk might benefit from an editor from the Emerald Isle.

"Samuel Beckett is the finest science fiction editor in America!"

83

Kornbluth declared. Beckett gestured surreptitiously for silence, which neither the reporter nor Kornbluth saw. "Save for his two magazines" (Pohl frowned here) "modern science fiction is mere . . ." He groped for a word.

"Scatchophily," volunteered Lowndes, who had gotten through the book's easiest chapter.

"Scatch o' who?" the reporter asked. "And who might he be?"

"Unpack it yourself," said Blish. "I see 'scatophily,' which your Latin teacher must have taught you. Also, at a stretch, 'sci-fi.'" A few of his fellows snickered.

There was a commotion at the gangplank. The passengers, waving gaily and exclaiming over the crowd gathered below, were being allowed to disembark. Beckett walked along the railing, looking at them lined along the deck. He scarcely noticed the Futurians trailing behind him.

They were near the front, perhaps granted precedence owing to the two invalids in the party. Joyce was supported by his blind man's cane, thin and shockingly worn. His bespectacled eyes moved over the face of the crowd as though seeking the source of its sound. Nora, beside him, held an arm but was twisting to look back at Lucia, who proved the real shocker. Two men on either side of her (her brothers? Beckett could not remember), she glared at the crowd like a Christian facing the lions, her face a carven basilisk's. Looking at her extremity of impotence and pain, Beckett felt his heart contract into a stone.

The rustle in the crowd increased as the Joyce party moved gravely down the plank. Flashbulbs popped, and Joyce flinched and raised a hand to his eyes.

A party had gathered at the bottom to meet them. Beckett, seeking to get closer, found his way blocked by jostling journalists, but could see fitfully over their heads. At the center of the tumult, Mr. Bennett Cerf was stepping forward to shake Joyce's hand.

Lucia's gaze ranged angrily over the crowd, and Beckett thought for a heart-stopping second that she had recognized him. Beckett stepped back and was about to turn away when he felt the reporter grasp his elbow.

"Let's go," he said, pulling him firmly forward. Beckett began to protest, but the reporter propelled him briskly through the crowd, calling "Make way" and "Friend of the family here" in a voice that compelled compliance. In a minute the two tall Irishmen were within six feet of the Joyces.

Nora saw them first, and stared at Beckett with an expression that flickered through bemusement, startled recognition, and alarm. She spoke rapidly with one of her sons and Lucia was taken by the arm and led quickly away. Beckett felt a lance of pain spear through him.

She had evidently said something to Joyce, for he turned his head alertly. "Sam?" he said, his fine tenor quavery.

"I'm here." A lump like a boiled potato rose in his throat.

The two men clasped each other awkwardly by the forearms, Joyce peering owlishly into Beckett's impassive face. A few more flashbulbs popped.

"Are you fat and sassy in Neue Amsterdam, then?"

"Ah, we eat high on the hog here, and the pubs are open all day." Beckett looked at the ravaged face with emotions too roiled to sort.

"And are you still editing those newsstand magazines?"

"Oh, yes. Got a story from Lord Dunsany last year, and a ghostly tale by Frank O'Connor."

"We are hoping, Mr. Joyce, to publish extracts from *your* next novel," said Kornbluth suddenly.

"Eh?" Joyce looked about for the source of the new voice.

Blushing furiously, Beckett introduced the Futurians. "Four young American writers," he said, stressing the second word.

"Mamalujo," said Joyce, amused. He turned to them. "And why would my work be of interest to a fantasy magazine?"

"'Comehome to roo, wee chickchilds doo, when the wildworewolf's abroad.'" That was Blish, speaking up bravely.

Passengers streaming off the boat were pressing against the knot surrounding Joyce, who was being jostled steadily outward. Beckett found himself being pushed away from them and struggled to keep close without shoving back. Joyce's frail voice was frayed by the shuffling tumult. ". . . My next novel, a seasong and paean to the land where most men of Irish blood now live, to be called . . ."

"What did he say?" Beckett demanded.

"Sounded like 'The latter, the latter,'" said Pohl.

"I thought it was 'The Letter,'" said Kornbluth.

85

A microphone was being held before Joyce, who obligingly raised his voice slightly. "I am delighted to be in the United States, the first English-speaking country to publish my *Ulysses* and the one in which I have been most ably championed. It is a deliverance to make landfall in a country that has thrown off the dead but heavy hand of those blue-pencilling bluenoses, John and Emma Bull . . ."

He was borne away on a tide of serge. Becket stood, the Futurian juveniles clustered about him like pups, as his wounded king was escorted into exile. A fled Fool, established but unfattened in the land of silk and money, he watched as the retinue vanished from sight, leaving him clutching the ink-smudged ribbons of a public's tawdry dreams.

Nick DiChario hadn't been in print a year when he found himself nominated for a Hugo, a Campbell, and a WFC Award. He's sold about 20 stories in less than 3 years, and clearly remembers a Challenger flight that most of us missed.
—M.R.

MISSION 51-L

Nicholas A. DiChario

1. Countdown!

Lyndon B. Johnson Space Center,
Houston, Texas,
December, 1985.

All of us journalism undergrads crowd into the IR (interviewing room) along with the regular press corps, awaiting our first crack at the Hugo winners.

For me, after four days of touring the JSC (Johnson Space Center), the excitement of my assignment has waned, and I'm beginning to see what a life of reporting may someday hold for me: Lots of waiting around for somebody to say something enthralling, and then making somebody *sound* enthralling when he isn't. So I've made the acquaintance of a bespectacled young fellow of like mind named Butch, from a community college somewhere in West Virginia, and as soon as the DB (debriefing) is over we'll be heading down NASA Road 1 to the FC (Flight Club) to discuss the pros and cons of our questionable career choice.

My name is Nick DiChario. I'm enrolled at the State University of New York, Manhattan, in their undergraduate journalism program, and I've been invited to JSC along with a few hundred other journalism students from across the country as part of NASA's good-will effort to involve the academic community in Mission 51-L, SF-writer-in-space.

The IR is a cream-colored, eggshell of a room with an oval table up front, and chairs for the NASA people. It smells sterile and looks scrubbed, like everything else at JSC. I hang back and watch the

Harvards and Yalies wrestle for the non-assigned seats near the platform. A door swings open in the front corner of the IR, and the candidates file into the room, to cameras snapping and reporters shouting questions.

Gibson, Varley, Butler, and Brin wave and smile and take their seats on the rostrum, along with some guy, obviously NASA brass, older fellow in his sixties who I assume will be running the show. Next to Gibson sits another man, very big, gotta be six-two, two-eighty, stringy hair and beard, wearing glasses and a plaid flannel shirt. Right away I nudge Butch. "Who's Grizzly Adams?" Butch shrugs. The other candidates are dressed smartly in their sky-blue NASA fatigues. I flip open my notepad and ready my pen. This might be the only action I get for weeks.

"I want to thank you all for coming," says the balding NASA guy. He grins and waits for the commotion to settle. "We only have a few minutes, so is there anyone who would like to ask a question of our candidates?"

Mistake. Several hundred questions fire from the launch pad at once. The bald guy tries to ferret out at least one. Maybe he does, or maybe he just makes up one of his own: "All right," he says, speaking loudly into the microphone, "the question is, how do each of the candidates feel about their chances of being selected for the flight?"

The room quiets, except for papers shuffling, pens scratching, a cough here and there, and anxious press people fidgeting in their seats. I pull out my press kit: Hugo Winners / SF-writer-in-space Finalists / *Only one will fly*!

William Gibson, Year's Best Novel: *Neuromancer*.

John Varley, Year's Best Novella: "Press Enter."

Octavia Butler, Year's Best Novelette: "Bloodchild."

David Brin, Year's Best Short Story: "The Crystal Spheres."

The committee has provided us with photographs, in-depth bios prepared by NASA's public relations liaisons, and some excerpts from the candidates' award-winning fiction. I've always considered myself a science-fiction reader—I've even written a couple of clumsy, unpublished short stories—but I've never heard of any of these authors.

"I feel very good about my chances," says Brin. "I'm excited about the opportunity, and I'm looking forward to the training."

"It's an honor just to be nominated—eh, considered," says

Varley, a tall, unassuming man.

Gibson nods slowly, as if contemplating each phase of the nod. He hasn't stopped crossing and re-crossing his legs or playing with his glass of water since he sat down. It's almost as if his body is nervous, but his head doesn't know it yet.

"I think I have the best chance," says Butler. "Let's face it, I'm a woman, and I'm a black. NASA has the opportunity to honor two historically oppressed minorities with one grand gesture. They'd be insane not to pick me."

That answer brings the press corps to its feet, hollering follow-ups. Butch glances at me and smiles. I give him the old NASA thumbs-up and jot down her answer. The bald guy in the uniform grins, but I can tell he's being selective about the questions now. He lets everybody have at it for a good twenty seconds. Then he turns to the candidates and says, "I think I heard somebody ask about you, Mr. Shepard. Why don't you introduce yourself to the press?" Mr. Shepard? He's not supposed to be a finalist, but I've seen that name somewhere. I skim through my packet. Ah, Shepard, Lucius. Nominated for two Hugo Awards this year, but not a winner.

"I'm Lucius Shepard," says Shepard. "Hugo nominee. Someone from the Selection Committee called me up yesterday and invited me to this shindig, so here I am. Don't know why, but I guess I'm in the running."

"Come now, Mr. Shepard," says Butler. She's got a very precise, deep, sexy voice. She's right about one thing. NASA would be insane not to pick her. "It doesn't take much thinking to figure out why you're here."

I elbow Butch. "We're gonna like this Butler lady. She's good press."

"Two nominations is as good as one win," says Gibson, his first words, and he looks damned proud of them. Shepard smiles and pats him on the back.

"Nonsense," says Butler. "You're here because you're a better stylist than all of us put together." She states this matter-of-factly, then sips from her glass of ice water. "The committee brought you here because they're hoping you'll win this competition. They're salivating over the possibility of getting even a few paragraphs from your pen about what it's like to be up there, in space." She nods toward the ceiling. "I can't say as I blame them. But in the end, it won't do you any good. They'll still have to pick me for who I am, and for what I stand for. Unless I drop dead, it's a foregone conclusion."

"Wow!" says Butch. "I'm in love with that oppressed, black, female, sci-fi writer!"

"You'll have to stand in line, my friend," I tell him. "What was that last line?"

"She says it's a foregone conclusion."

"Right, got it."

Brin stifles his anger, leans forward. "Well, now, I wouldn't be too sure about that. If the NASA people had already made up their minds, they would have simply picked one of us. We all need to go through the paces. The one who trains the best will go, I'm certain. Space travel is nothing to fool around with. You have to be physically and mentally fit."

"That leaves me out," says Shepard. He leans back, pats his belly, and crosses his eyes. (He's wearing a pair of thick glasses that magnifies the eye-crossing effect.) Everybody laughs except Brin. I can tell already Brin won't make the final cut. He's too uptight. Gibson, he's out, too weird for words. Varley has a slim chance if he holds up under training—tall, handsome, confident, under-stated—but he'll have to walk on water to beat Butler. A few more routine questions and answers, and our big moment has passed. "That's all for today, folks," says baldy.

I pocket my pen, stand up, and glance at Butch. "One good thing about sitting in the back —

"Yes," Butch agrees, clapping shut his notepad. "Last at the press conference, first at the Flight Club."

And the two of us are off to the pub.

2. The Opprobrious Stuff!

Hell week for the WIS (writer-in-space) candidates:

On the treadmill test, Brin and Varley and Butler all score miserably low. Gibson performs well, but NASA physicians express concern when he suggests direct-implant brainmicrobionics might enhance his performance. (The physicians make note of this for the

NASA psychiatrist.)

The spatial disorientation chair, better known as the "vomit comet" (quoting press kit here) , is intended to simulate the feeling of weightlessness in space. It spins so fast that the world becomes an "exaggerated blur" to the test subjects. The only one to survive it without walking into walls for the rest of the day is Gibson, who seems oddly invigorated by the experience. (The physicians make note of this for the NASA psychiatrist.) The altitude chamber is used to guage the effects of hypoxia on crew members. An oxygen deficiency can lead to distorted vision, nausea, a tingling of the extremities, and "abnormalities or exaggerated tendencies of personality" (press kit again). The five of them sit crushed and sealed inside this chamber and soar to a simulated thirty-thousand feet.

When the technicians stop the ride and open the hatch, Butler is caught with her hand between Shepard's legs, Brin and Varley are trying to yank out each other's nose hairs, and Gibson reports an "odd but illuminating sense of euphoria," (another note for the psych file).

And so it goes for the next few weeks: motion sickness, hyperventilation, loss of equilibrium, decompression syndrome, psychological distress. Varley, during the crash simulation drills on the mock-up shuttle, presses enter when he shouldn't and destroys a two-million-dollar flight panel. Gibson is caught panty-raiding Butler's quarters at 2:30 in the morning. Brin insults Shepard's girth when Shepard has trouble squeezing through a shuttle passage, and spends a day apologizing in front of the press. "Shep and I go way back," he says, "no harm done." To which Shepard replies, "Why did the Brin cross the road? Because his #@@%&*! got stuck in the chicken."

I get tired of it in a hurry—following them around, scribbling down their every utterance, hoping they'll either screw up or say something quotable, or better yet unquotable. Hell of a way to make a living.

The Flight Club, on the other hand, offers several varieties of bottled beer, and going boldly where I've naught gone before, I discover Killian's Red. Butch is a Bud man all the way, and as I'm trying to convince him to live a little, Lucius Shepard walks in and plops down on a bar stool. I glance at my wrist watch: 10:34 AM.

"What the hell is Shepard doing here at this hour of the morning?"

Butch looks up from his game of table-top Pac Man and raises his Bud. "What the hell are we doing here?"

"Good point. C'mon." I set aside *Sports Illustrated's* Chicago/New England Super Bowl preview issue, we pick up our press packets and our frosty mugs, and head for the end of the bar. "Mr. Shepard," I say. "My name is Nick. This is my friend, Butch. Can we buy you a—" it suddenly occurs to me that the WIS candidates might not be allowed to drink—

"You don't have to buy me anything. I've just ordered a Gentleman Jack, and NASA is picking up the tab on my personal expense account. But you're welcome to join me."

Butch and I hop up on the bar stools flanking Shepard. We're surrounded by dozens of photos of astronauts, a giant mural of the Mercury Capsule, and right up over the beer taps a black-and-white of John F. Kennedy with the words *Profile in Courage* inscribed on a shiny pewter plaque. The television is tuned to MTV, Michael Jackson's *Thriller*.

"We're here with the student press," says Butch.

Shepard smirks. "The pocket protectors are a dead giveaway."

Butch and I quickly remove them. "We picked them up at the JSC souvenir shop," I tell him, "just for laughs."

Up close, Shepard's got a real amiable look about him: cheeks like Georgia peaches, soft eyes, a cleft chin under his beard, dewy perspiration across his forehead that gives him the air of a gentleman farmer. The bartender puts down a loaded shot glass that looks like a mini-space-helmet, circa '69.

"Ah," says Shepard, "space petrol of the gods."

"What are you doing here?" asks Butch. "I mean, aren't you supposed to be in training today? Tomorrow's the big announcement."

Shepard gulps his Jack without a wince. "I've got an appointment at eleven-hundred-hours with NASA's psychiatrist, where I fully intend to nuke whatever remote possibility I still might have of going up in that death-trap shuttle."

"Death-trap shuttle? What do you mean? It says here . . . Butch flips through his press kit. "It says here you'll be flying with one of NASA's most accomplished crews, led by Commander Dick Scobee, and that the *Challenger* is the darling of NASA's shuttle fleet."

Shepard laughs. "Let me tell you something about that little darling. It goes from zero to the speed of sound in literally sixty seconds. It's fueled by a mixture of pure liquid oxygen and hydrogen and has a cruising speed of seventeen-thousand miles-per-hour. That contraption can skip across Europe in less time than it takes you to piss that beer. Doesn't that kind of power *scare* you?"

"Well, sure," says Butch. "I'm just surprised it scares you."

"Common sense," Shepard says. "The *Challenger* has been through more missions and has flown more miles than any other shuttle, its tile-integrity is suspect, NASA aborted its next to last mission due to an engine failure, it has suffered a cracked fuel line, and once came within three seconds—count 'em, one, two, three—of becoming an incendiary in space when hot gases nearly burned clean through to a rocket booster. Not to mention no shuttle has ever flown this heavy a payload, four-and-a-half-million-pounds. You'd have to be a nut to climb in that casket. No, sir. I've enjoyed my stay, but now it's time to move on, however ungraciously."

Butch is still fumbling through his press kit. "But it says here there is only a one in one million chance of a fatal space shuttle accident."

"That's NASA's study," says Shepard. "An independent federal review came up with one in one-thousand, and the Air Force's own people said one in thirty-five."

"You're kidding," I say.

Shepard grins. "You won't find that in the ol' press kit."

Butch frowns. "If you feel that way, why did you accept NASA's invitation in the first place?"

"Free transportation," Shepard answers. "Free food and lodging for a month, the national attention can't hurt my career, and lots of stuff I've never done before."

"What makes you think you can whitewash the psychiatrist?" I ask him. "I hear she's a pretty tough old bird."

Shepard motions the bartender for another shot. "Have you ever read any of my stories?"

I'm embarrassed to say no, so I just shake my head.

"If you had, you wouldn't be asking."

Butch chuckles.

"But I like science-fiction," I tell him. "I've even written a couple

93

of stories. Unpublished." I've never revealed that to anyone, and I'm kind of surprised it pops out now.

"Let me guess," says Shepard. "You've read Asimov's *Foundation* trilogy, and Clarke's *Childhood's End?*"

"Hey, yeah, how did you know? I really enjoyed them. And the *Dune* series, too."

"You've got a long way to go, kid."

"What advice do you have for a budding young author?"

"Read some Shepard." He throws back his shot and smacks his lips. "I'd better get going." He motions to the bartender. "Two brews for my pals, here," he says, "on NASA." And then he walks out.

❀

It's the afternoon before the *Challenger* launch, we've been summoned into a huge auditorium, and the press is itching for the big news. The place reeks of sweat. The air conditioner is working so hard against the Houston heat that I can hear it rasping like a wounded bear somewhere up above the ceiling tiles.

Butch and I entertain a friendly wager. I say NASA is bound to pick Octavia Butler. I see no reason to doubt her black-oppressed-female-sci-fi-writer logic. Butch says they brought in Shepard for a reason, and even if we don't know what it is yet (even if *Shepard* doesn't know what it is yet) we'll find out soon enough. We've got an all-you-can-drink night at the Flight Club riding on this, and since today is Super Bowl Sunday, that could turn into a hefty tab, so when conference time rolls around I'm more than a little curious for the outcome.

The candidates file into the aud. A standing ovation greets Butler, Brin, Gibson, Varley, and Shepard. They're all pretty smug. Why not? If nothing else, they've survived.

The old bald guy in the uniform sits down and picks up the microphone. "Good day, everyone, I'm sure you're all anxious to find out who will be going up in space!"

Cheering, clapping, feet stomping, whistling, flashbulbs popping, some people waving American flags. It brings back the good ol' days of pride in the American Space Program. Even I have to admit this is pretty exciting stuff. History in the making, and all.

"First off," says baldy, "all the candidates are to be commended for their efforts and achievements during the training process. It's

94

not easy, and we here at NASA did not hold back. These people went through the same regimen as our regular astronauts."

More clapping. The candidates smile and congratulate one another. Shepard looks especially pleased with himself. I don't know what he said to the NASA psychiatrist, but rumor has it the old girl needed to be revived with smelling salts after he left the room.

"And now for the announcement you've all been waiting for." The bald guy stands up and says, "The first civilian science-fiction writer to travel in space will be. . Harlan Ellison!"

Stunned silence.

A short guy wearing Calvin Klein blue-jeans and a red silk smoking jacket strides through the door and out onto the platform. He's got a pipe in his mouth, although it's not lit, and he's wearing a navy-blue NASA baseball cap. "Thank you," he says. "Thank you very much."

The press corps explodes with questions. You can tell none of the other science-fiction writers had any idea this was coming. Dumbfounded expressions, mouths agape. Brin actually stands up and says, "What the fuck is this?" (I can't hear him above the din, but I can see his lips form the words.)

Butch leans over and shouts in my ear, "What the fuck is this?"

I shrug. "A push," I yell, thinking of our bet.

He nods. "To the FC!"

"We can read about all this in the newspapers tomorrow." I slap shut my notepad and head for the exit. The sooner we get to the club, the better our seats for the Super Bowl.

3. Liftoff!

Press Release from NASA's Selection Committee, June '85:

[*". . . It is only proper that we give back to the science fiction community that which they have prophesied, that which they have believed in and strove for in thought, in word, and in film, long before the scientific capability of space flight ever existed. .. . In recognition of their contributions and their undying vision, the first private citizen in space will be a science-fiction writer . . ."*]

Apparently, when this whole concept of SFWIS was born back

in June of '85, there is never any doubt in the minds of NASA brass that Harlan Ellison is their man. To divert national attention from Ellison as he prepares for his flight, they come up with this elaborate Hugo hoax. It's a pretty cruel trick to play on the others, I think, (some say it was Ellison's brainstorm), but the candidates are "duly compensated," (I'm quoting the *Washington Post* here) and none of them, not even Brin, complain about the remuneration.

Butch and Lucius Shepard and I watch liftoff from the FC along with the other students who couldn't come up with the plane fare, or couldn't clear a flight to Kennedy. We are fairly bleary-eyed, having sloshed our way through the Bears dismantling of the Pats, 46-10, in a football game about as exciting as a proctology exam.

On TV, launch pad 39-B erupts, and the Challenger blasts toward the heavens, leaving a seven-hundred-foot trail of smoke and conflagration behind it.

Then, suddenly, WHAP!, the dot on screen snaps into a flaming match stick. Vapor trails stream across the sky through a burgeoning, ivory, mushroom of smoke, and the cheers of only a moment ago turn to silent horror.

"It's exploded," someone says, well past the time we've all figured it out for ourselves.

"Shit," says Shepard, "I guess this means no *Last Dangerous Visions*."

The news teams scramble to get confirmation from MCC (mission control center) , and slowly the facts sift through: Trouble seventy-three seconds into the flight. Fifty-thousand feet over the Atlantic Ocean, *Challenger* has burst into fiery debris. Mission 51-L is a disaster. Lost. All is lost. No possibility of survivors.

Shepard asks the bartender for another shot, and raises his glass toward the television set. "Here's to Harlan," he toasts. "He's finally done it."

"Done what?" I ask.

Then some kid, I think he might be a Yalie, falls to his knees and starts crying right there in the middle of the club: "Ellison is god!" he shrieks. "Ellison is god!"

❋

"It's inevitable, you know, this science-fiction thing. Asimov and Clarke pull you in, and then all of a sudden you're hooked for life." (I'm quoting Shepard here.) Before we leave Houston, Lucius

96

invites me to his place in New York City for some pointers, anytime I can clear my schedule. As it turns out, we only live a few miles from each other.

When I get home to Manhattan there is an envelope awaiting me from *Worlds Beyond* magazine. Truth sometimes really is stranger than fiction. On the very day of the *Challenger* tragedy, I sell my first SF story to a semi-prozine for half-a-penny-a-word. A beginning.

I know in my heart I'm about as cut out for the news media as Gibson is for an ambassadorship to Guam, so I pick up Shepard's *Green Eyes* at the local Walden's, lock myself in my room, and start reading. After Shepard, I'm going to read the Hugo winners, followed closely by Ellison. By then I ought to have a clue as to just how far I have to go.

Then I'll be ready to take up Shepard on that weekend. Maybe even sooner than he thinks.

The inordinately energetic eluki bes shahar is an editorial staffer for a major mass-market publisher and the author of several SF novels under her own name, as well as several more in other genres under a variety of pseudonyms. Here she offers a tale which may be perfectly introduced with that venerable workhorse of pulp-magazine intros: "Be careful what you ask for . . . you just might get it!"

–P.N.H.

MY OBJECT ALL SUBLIME
eluki bes shahar

The real trouble with being perfectly situated and perfectly comfortable, as Wynton Marchand had always suspected, was that it left you with too much free time. And leisure has never generated contentment; ask any ancient Greek or Roman.

Being a fan, Wynton was never content. Being an editor, he had no free time. And so he should have been protected from existential malaises of the spirit, but he wasn't.

And he shouldn't have gone to Selenecon, but he did.

Selenecon (pronounced, classically enough, Seleen-E-Con) was the largest SF Convention still located within a day-trip of New York. When Wynton had been a young fan, it had still been held within NYC itself, and the tales of its destruction of downmarket New York hotels was the stuff of Selenite legend. Now that Wynton was a Filthy Pro, a Senior Editor at Bedlam Books (named for its owner, Thomas O. Bedlam), Selenecon was held in the wilds of, alternately, New Jersey and upstate New York, hosted by unwary hoteliers who had not yet heard the tales.

Or, perhaps, had heard them and didn't care.

The Hotel Escher was located in an area of Westchester County that had hit economic rock bottom when IBM left. Five hundred SF fans could do what they liked: they could not equal the damage done by the recession. And so this year, once again, the St. Patrick's Day weekend saw it filled almost to capacity with the few, the proud, the cream of New York's SF fan-and-prodom and their associated life forms, such as the publishing world.

Including, even and inevitably, SF editors.

Wynton Marchand gazed down at the program book in his hand, looking for the location of the panel that commanded his presence in half an hour's time. Not even the sight of two reasonably comely femfen in skin-tight *Next Generation* uniforms could lighten his mood. If anything, they darkened it: Wynton Marchand was allergic to Media SF in all of its forms.

"They've ruined everything," he muttered.

"Well, what do you expect—it's Selenecon," Lorne said. Like Wynton, he also worked for Bedlam, but Lorne peacefully edited Andiron, Bedlam's non-SF imprint. As a result, he looked upon these conventions as vacation.

"No," said Wynton, "that's not what I meant. The *Trekkies* have ruined everything. Look at this," he went on, brandishing the program at Lorne. "Panels on *Star Trek*—panels on *sex*—panels on those gawdawful Futuristic Romances—and romantic Vampires—and umpteen-book disposable interchangeable fantasy series written by fat Radcliffe graduates. *Where's the SF?*"

"In the dealer's room?" Lorne suggested hopefully, attempting to stave off an explosion. Though Marchand's name was frequently linked with his spiritual forebear and preceptor, John W. Campbell, Lorne did not feel it was quite so necessary to follow the ways of the Great Man in all things.

But the predicted explosion did not come. Wynton merely swelled up like an aggrieved blowfish. "I've been there. Fantasy, roleplaying game tie-in books, and *Star Trek* books. That's where it all started, you know—*Star Trek*," he said sorrowfully.

But a sorrowful Wynton was in some ways harder to deal with than a Wynton enraged. Lorne hastily announced himself desirous of seeing the panel on Fantasy Universe Crossovers that was starting in five minutes, and left.

On his way, he delivered a parting shot. Perhaps it was an attempt to be pacifying, but you never know.

"Well, at least you don't have that problem these days; these days they're all home in front of their VCR's," Lorne said. "That's where Marcia is now."

※

"The so-called Fantasy genre as it exists today is as formula-driven as the worst of the pulps, and, like some species of sub-literary kudzu, has expanded to the point that it has driven the worthwhile books off the racks," Wynton said firmly, and reached for his water glass. "We can hope that history will only regard this outbreak as a regrettable and temporary blip," he added, forcing a smile.

The panel was titled—as it had been every year for the last twenty years—"New Trends In SF". Wynton's comments were more in the nature of a hopeful prophecy than a prediction of a trend.

"That 'blip' is eleven percent of the book-buying dollar," Elaine MacGregor said from the other end of the table. Elaine was the SF buyer for the biggest of the national chains, and unfortunately, Elaine *liked* fantasy. "SF isn't even on the map," she added.

"What about *Star Trek* books?" someone piped up—predictably—from the audience. "They're always on the bestseller lists."

"What about that, Frank?" Elaine said, deftly passing the conversational ball to Frank Levine, who had written twenty *Star Trek* books and looked good for twenty more.

"Well, *Trek* is SF of a sort," Levine said, "and I've always felt—as you'll see if you read my *The Medusa Conundrum—*"

Wynton tuned them all out.

He didn't remember the rest of the panel. He knew it by heart, anyway—more tired excuses, pretending they didn't know the truth: that SF was being wiped out.

It was *Star Trek* that did it, of course, though not alone. But all the Trekkies who'd flooded into SF fandom, expecting it to be just like the Starship Enterprise, were the iceberg tip of the audience who bought with such voracious appetite endless books about girl witches and their pet dragons.

Was Lorne right? Would they all go away now that they could stay home and simply re-run tapes of their favorite television pap endlessly? Lorne's girlfriend was a Trekkie; he could be expected to know.

But even if it were true, it would come too late to save SF.

The Hotel Escher was suddenly too hot, the Selenites too oblivious. Wynton got into his car and headed back for the city.

❋

He didn't quite realize where he was going until he pulled into the lot on 53rd street and looked up at the Art Deco facade of the building at the end of the block. He'd been going home, of course,

100

and home for the last 25 years had been the thirteenth floor offices of Bedlam Books. He crossed the lobby, entered one of the famed hydraulic elevators (the last in the city) and pushed the button for home.

The doors opened on the thirteenth floor, painted its familiar gas chamber green. There were even a few other people here—though mostly from sales and marketing, areas that had become more and more important as the actual intellectual content of books disappeared. Marchand despised them all—they'd reduced publishing to a series of pre-sold sound bites, signifying nothing.

Wynton breathed a sigh of relief as he reached his office sanctuary. It was filled, of course, with the books and manuscripts that were any editor's workload, but there was more: the Best Fanzine Hugo that Wynton's *SquaLour* had won in 1965; badges from Worldcons stretching back into SF's Silver Age; the Hogu that Bedlam Books had garnered for the infamous "Real Fake Book" Hoax of 1974. These were the touchstones of Wynton's life; his benchmarks.

His sense of reality restored by these familiar talismans, Wynton turned to his desk. Might as well do some work, now that he was here. He ought to go back to the convention for the evening; Bedlam was throwing a publisher's party and everyone would expect to see him. But if he put in a few hours now it would be that much less for later. And there was always later. Every one he met seemed to have a manuscript in submission, and every single one of them was fantasy.

The towering, teetering pile upon his desk was made up of the hopefuls from the slushpile, as referred to him by his assistant Denise. Denise had the makings of a good editor someday—and a real love for SF, even if she did confuse it with *Star Trek*.

Wynton Marchand sat down at his desk, and reached for the synopsis lying on the top of the pile. He picked it up and read:

"Young F'Ret-Ree-Kcher of the Chatagatoar did not realize that she was fated to become the most powerful of the feline sorcerer-queens of fabled Mhoggimuur—"

He felt a faint despairing inevitability creep over him. It was true that he could not be certain what the entire pile held. It was also certain that he could not avoid knowing. His flight from the convention had bought him only a temporary respite from the world as it was.

There was no escape.

101

✳

"There is simply no escape," Wynton said at the Selenite's Wednesday meeting the following week. His relationship with the Selenite Science Fiction Club, like his relationship with SF fandom as a whole, was adversarial at best, but at least the Selenites held the line: no mediafen or romance writers ever darkened the doorways of the Selenites' Wednesday night meetings.

"There is no problem so large that it cannot be run away from," Elkanah Wright—known as Elk—assured him. Elk was a Selenite in the old mold: a graduate student of ambiguous researches and inexplicit income.

"You're wrong," Wynton assured him gravely. He took another pull on his beer—it was left over from the Dublin in '05 bid party at the convention, and so it was green, but that didn't matter. "There's no place to go. History has taken a wrong turn."

"The time is out of joint, eh?" Elk said, sitting down. Of all the Selenites, he was the only one who had never approached Wynton with a story, or an idea for a story, and Wynt was profoundly grateful.

"Well, there's a cure for that." Elk never drank anything stronger than water; he had a tall glass of seltzer in his hand as he spoke.

"A time machine?" Wynton had had three beers since he'd gotten here and two double Scotches before he arrived; he felt the lucid ability to follow any conversational thread effortlessly. "Ah, if I had a time machine, I know what I'd do."

"What's that?"

Elk seemed unusually interested, even for a Selenite, that subspecies of a tribe that carried rapacious curiosity to new extremes. It made Wynt think better of explaining.

"I'd use it," he said briefly.

Elk smiled.

"Well, I don't have a time machine. But I've got a Chronoleptic Pantograph. That's almost as good."

Wynton'd had too many beers to remember what -leptic, as a suffix, meant. Sleep? Chrono was "time", of course, and "Pantograph" was part of the title of an unpublished Alexi Panshin novel.

"Almost as good," he said. "A time machine."

"No," said Elk patiently, and explained again. In detail.

By the time he was finished, Wynton was close to sober and

102

convinced that he was being suckered into a hoax of galactic magnitude.

"And let me guess," he said, when Elk was finished, "you've got this Dean Drive gizmo, and you'll sell it to me. Am I right?"

"No," said the Elk, "but I'll rent it to you."

He would, as it happened, demonstrate it before he rented it. On the basis of the demonstration, Wynton Marchand agreed to the enormous fee necessary to rent the Pantograph for one month of unlimited use.

Wynton's fatal flaw had always been that he preferred the hard SF of Asimov, Clarke, and Niven—even Heinlein—to the work of more ambiguous writers. Had he only listened to Kuttner, or Sturgeon, or Leiber, he might have saved himself.

But he hadn't, so he didn't.

It took him a year to make his preparations, but Wynton Marchand finally had all the time in the world. His colleagues commented approvingly on the change in him—he even bought multiple-volume fantasies featuring spunky girl wizards without complaint—and Wynton smiled onward. He sold his car, he cashed in his life insurance, he maxed his plastic, and he took out a loan in preparation for his journey. Some of the things he bought were very expensive. Some were ridiculously cheap. Some were illegal, though not immoral. And some were merely hard to find.

If I had a time machine, I know what I'd do.

And then he took a month's vacation.

The rules governing the Chronoleptic Pantograph were simple, Elk had told him. You went to the same place you left from and returned to the future exactly as much time after you left as you had spent in the past. Wynton's parents had been in Europe in 1965. He set the Pantograph for that year, positioned everything he needed on the induction grid, stood in his living room, and—jaunted.

He'd made inquiries in the past year, even to the heroic extent of taking Lorne and Marcia out to dinner. The results had been electrifying.

"Oh, sure, VCR's have almost killed real fandom," Marcia said, oblivious to the hidden agenda of her auditor. "Everybody's doing music videos now; no 'zines. When I came in there wasn't anything like that. All we had was the fanzines—and boy! did we have fanzines. It just isn't the same, now that you can tape every episode when it's first aired. Nobody does 'zines any more."

So, Wynton reflected afterward, *it was all true. If there were VCR's in 1966, there would be no Trekkies.*

An ordinary man, armed with the Chronoleptic Pantograph, would have taken a shipment of video cassette recorders back to 1966.

Wynton was cleverer than that.

He took only a few VCRs.

And he jaunted back to 1965.

The past was a foreign country; somewhere in it a 20-year-old Wynton Marchand stood on the threshold of his life, sure that he could bring his SFnal dreams to life. His elder *doppelganger* moved carefully, aware that he had only a month of days to make his dreams come true. But a great editor must be organized, and Wynton was one of the greats.

He rented a room—the rent was absurdly low—and jaunted slowly forward through the year, returning to the present between each forward skip, even if only for a few seconds, to keep the time from going too far out of joint, and to water his plants. He put the video cassette recorder into production from the carefully retrofitted blueprints he'd carried back with him, and the first locally-produced unit was assembled before he even filed his patent applications.

He could only afford production on a small scale, but he didn't care: just as he had hoped, his "new invention" was pirated early on, and a thousand competing models of VCR flooded the market. It didn't matter to Wynton. He didn't even bother to defend.

And so, as a result, when the first episode of a new series called *Star Trek* aired in September of 1966, any number of households across America were ready to tape it.

Just to be sure, Wynton taped it himself, hooking the bulky, vacuum-tubed VCR up to the television in his rented room. It was "The Incredible Salt Vampire" episode and while it wasn't particularly bad—for filmed science fiction—it was the thin end of the wedge and Wynton abjured it.

He had five days left of his month, and spent them jaunting

forward, his stops months apart, making sure the past settled securely into its new channel. He even risked attending a Selenite meeting (praying he wouldn't be taken for his father). No one recognized him, but he found that each Wednesday's meeting now apparently began with a re-showing of the previous Thursday's *Star Trek*, much to Wynton's disgust. He saw Elk at the meeting, looking much the same as he would thirty years later—was it his imagination, or did Elk fix him with a knowing gaze?

Before Wynton left the past for the last time, he hired lawyers to defend his patent infringement case on a contingency basis, just for the look of the thing, but he didn't care if he won. He walked across town—the Chronoleptic Pantograph concealed under his coat—and let himself into the apartment that still, in this time, belonged to his parents.

And then he jaunted home.

He returned to realtime exactly the amount of time after he had left that he had spent in the past: a total of thirty days. It was early Monday morning; as one returning from a foreign country, Wynton savored the grey Apocalyptic babble of *fin de siecle* Manhattan, seen through the windows of the apartment that was now his. What agreeable wonders of redeemed literature lay beyond his door? Perhaps *Worlds of If* was still publishing, or *Galaxy*.

He repacked the Chronoleptic Pantograph in its case and left a message on Elk's answering machine, and then, unable to contain himself, went down to Bedlam. He would go to *Forbidden Planet* afterward, he promised himself, and bask in the sunshine of a world without elves, unicorns, or trilogies.

He reached Bedlam Books afire with the vision of the new authors he would be able to read; the science fiction that there now was room for on the shelves and the publisher's lists; the unpublished, undiscovered masters and journeymen that now, in this brave new world, would achieve the recognition they deserved.

The first shock came when the elevator doors opened.

The corridor was painted pink.

It was the week before ABA; there were promo pieces everywhere, but they didn't say "Bedlam's Books are Bonnie" or "Through Bedlam To the Stars" or "It's not a book— It's Bedlam" or any of their other advertising taglines.

They said: "Chantilly *Lace* is a Brand New Face".

"Hi, Wynt! Good to see you back." Denise, looking blessedly normal, greeted him from behind the receptionist's desk, her frequent early morning haunt. Behind her were the massed shelves of output for Bedlam's current season.

No. Not Bedlam. *Chantilly*.

Only a few books on the shelves were familiar; Bedlam had always done westerns and technothrillers, and those were here. But all the rest said "Chantilly" on the spine. All of them seemed to be by women named Catharine or Nicole and had three-world-long semantically interchangeable titles.

"What . . . *is* this?" Wynton demanded hoarsely.

Denise smiled, thinking he meant the standups. "Do you like it? They're for the spin-off of the new Chantilly line—*Lace* is for the independent, non-career-oriented woman who likes a lifestyle of drama and adventure. We've got—"

"You must be mad," Wynton informed her.

Denise peered at him cautiously. "Are you sure you're feeling all right? Maybe a little too much vacation? Didn't you read your mail?"

"What?"

Denise got up from behind the desk and came over to him. "Maybe you'd better sit down for a while, Wynt. We've got the launch meeting for *Lace* at ten, and you know the editor hasn't been named yet, but everyone knows that Tom's probably going to pick you, and we wouldn't want to do anything to spoil that, now, would we?" she said, as coaxingly as if he were a fractious child.

This was not, Wynton thought weakly, what he had intended.

Denise led him down the hall, past bookcases filled with books in every shade of pink and orange and purple, past doors trimmed with Valentine hearts and lace and pictures of nearly-naked men.

"After all, Romance *is* 84% of the market these days, and you *are* the best. Ever since Rosemary Rodgers practically made romance with *Sweet Savage Love* in '72 and we finally realized that you'd been right all along about that *Star Trek* of yours—the women's market for futuristic relationship fiction could be even bigger—remember? Even if it is a little radical to have a man editing it, I know you could make

Lace a success."

They stopped in front of his door and Denise opened it. Did the Hugo look a little smaller, the Worldcon badges more faded?

He'd sworn to himself he would not ask, but in the end he could not help himself.

"Denise, what about Science Fiction?"

A chill slid into his heart as he watched her try to place the reference, but at last her brow cleared. "Oh, don't you worry—Tom won't take those away from you, even if you are doing *Lace*. It'll still be one book per list. Three a year, just like always. After all, how much more of that stuff could the market support, right?"

Wynton walked into his office as a man would ascend the gallows. Denise stood in the doorway for a moment, and then left.

The shelves were still filled with books he had done, the walls papered with covers, but he looked for familiar names in vain.

No Varley. No Niven. No Bear or Steele, Pournelle or Drake. The only Esther Friesner was a cover with the title *Sweet Savage Sorcerer*.

There was no SF. None.

What had Denise said? *"We finally realized that you'd been right all along about that* Star Trek *of yours—the women's market for futuristic relationship fiction could be even bigger than Rosemary Rodgers"*?

He had failed.

No, not even that. He had made it *worse*.

Slowly, Wynton sat down at his desk.

The VCR had not destroyed *Star Trek* fandom; it had let it blossom prematurely into an endless recycling of the imagined relationship between Kirk and Spock. *Star Trek* fans had not taken over SF fandom. They'd stayed home and written their endless stories, which hadn't had any connection with SF at all.

And when they'd bought books, they hadn't bought SF books. They'd bought romances.

He was still sitting when Denise brought him coffee and the *Post* a half hour later.

"I hope you feel better," Denise said tentatively.

"Sure," Wynton said, and meant it until he saw the headline: *"Moon Launch Scrubbed: NASA Back To Drawing Board"*

107

When he got back to his apartment the Pantograph was gone, of course, and Elk was no longer in the phone book. *Forbidden Planet* wasn't there either.

And Wynton Marchand was marooned forever in a world slowly turning pink.

Jack Haldeman is not only a top-notch skiffy author of long standing, but also a BNF (Big Name Fan). In fact, he chaired the 1974 Worldcon in Washington, D.C., though this story is about the Heinlein-Asimov feud that destroyed SFWA and almost ruined the 1968 Worldcon. You remember that one, right?

—M.R.

HISTORY LESSON
by Jack C. Haldeman II

*Being a true first-hand account of the Big Feud
between Robert Heinlein and Isaac Asimov, which
dissolved into a fist fight and turned the 1968
Worldcon into a fiasco, destroyed SFWA, and
changed the direction of an entire literary genre.*

No, I don't mind. Us old geezer ex-presidents of SFWA are always asked to reminisce about the old days. Dinosaur Panels, we call them. Piece of cake. Just put me on the stage, pass me a Heineken and a microphone. I'll talk all day. No problem.

I want to thank the committee for inviting me to speak here at Noreascon 12. There was a time I didn't think I'd make it past the year 2000, much less to be here to celebrate the 12th Boston Worldcon. Modern medicine is wonderful. But what you want to hear about is the Big Feud and how it changed Science Fiction forever.

I was there, you know. Of course it was before my pro days. I was fan. Hard core fan; pubbed me a zine, even put on a local con or two. I was plugged in.

Glorious days, they were. Halicon, even. I don't suppose you young fans would even recognize a mimeograph machine, much less a hecto. You got your Internet and your web-footed pages and RTCs and RAMs and all that, but we had trufannishness, born of ditto masters and LoCs and sticky quarters. I remember the smell of correction fluid and the thrill of opening a new box of mimeograph stencils; none of this typing the first thing that came into your mind, hitting return and sending it out though some fancy electric modem.

109

No, this was *real* communication printed on twenty pound golden-rod. It was meant to last, by golly, not like this babble-filled information superhighway.

But I digress. Is this microphone working?

Yes, I've seen fanzine collections that filled rooms. They were like shrines, you know. Most of you won't ever experience the thrill of holding a zine that was actually hand-cranked by Carr, Willis, Tucker. More's the pity, for our history is there, complete with strikeovers and illos.

But I digress. You wanted to hear about Asimov and Heinlein. Pass me another one of those Heinikins, would you?

It was Baycon, in the year of 1968. Yes, it all came down at the Worldcon in Oakland. Events transpired that brought both Heinlein and Asimov to that fateful and pivotal convention on a collision course that would shake the foundations of our strange land.

We had *cons* back then, let me tell you, real cons, not interactive multimedia events like this. I look over the crowd here and the only person I see wearing a propeller beanie is Dave Kyle. Oh, the shame, the shame.

Look, the total attendance at Oakland was 1,430, and that was considered huge at that time. But it was still small enough that most people knew everybody else. Sure, we had our SMOFs and our pros, but everybody just kind of mixed. It was rare indeed that anyone threw a closed party. Do that now, and you'll be out of beer in three minutes. We'd never heard of door dragons, nor had the need for them.

How many people are at this convention, Tony? I'm sure your wrist computer will give to an exact number. What's that . . . 23,478 you say? Yikes. It's only Friday. I rest my case.

We were family back then. We took care of our own. It was still possible to let your kids run around unattended and not have to worry. Theft was all but unheard of, and vandalism at a convention was unthinkable.

Like all families we had our share of squabbles, right from the beginning. There was the famous exclusion, of course; and the boondoggle was a very dark time. Hoaxes, too. Lord, did we have hoaxes. Fake personas would show up in the lettercols of fanzines all the time, usually spreading rumors, dissention and libel. It was great fun. Sometimes entire hoax fanzines showed up. Fake Worldcon bids were a biggie, too. A couple times they won.

But I digress. You don't want to hear about hoaxes, you want to hear about the Big Feud. But to understand the enormity of the event, you must understand how different our science fiction world was back in the 20th Century.

It was so different that you could actually find books in the dealer's room back then, and magazines, too. Used, even, or in mint condition—at a premium price—for the collectors. Now all I see are plastic movie figures and laser games. Of course, we called it the Huckster Room back then, but that was deemed not to be Politically Correct.

I hate that PC stuff. That killed nudity at the masquerade, which, by the way, we used to call a costume ball. We even had dancing. Real bands.

Nowadays the masquerade is so organized you have to fill out a stack of forms just to be prejudged to see if you get into the show. And dance? Forget it. I saw a woman wearing a hall costume yesterday with so much stuff hanging all over her you couldn't tell where the woman stopped and the tinfoil started. No way you could dance with that. Just as well, I suppose, since dancing these days seems to feature jumping off a stage and seeing how many people you can hurt. And if we had a band, it would probably sound like a car crash.

But I digress. You want to hear about the Big Feud.

I should have seen it coming, but truth to tell, I didn't.

It was the 60's. I was blinded by the stars. Heinlein, Asimov, Farmer, Silverberg.

I was blinded by a few other things, too. Remember, it was the San Francisco scene in the 60's and I was a young man. The Clarion Hotel was filled with the smell of incense and tear gas. Jerry Phipps kept feeding me "aspirin" that had a bunch of unexpected side effects like causing the walls to melt and neat-colored bugs to appear out of nowhere.

Have you ever *really* looked at your hands? Far out. All those fingers, and just the right number, too. What a marvelous concept hands are.

But I digress.

As I said, in order to understand the Big Feud, it needs to be put in historical perspective. Like the rest of the world, our commu-

111

nity was divided by the Vietnam War. We had our Hawks and Doves.

Peace symbols and love beads were thick as bees at that fateful Worldcon. So were buttons reading "America, Love It Or Leave It." I just love discourse. Of course there were arguments as well as reasoned discussion. Some of the arguments were quite heated, which lead to the occasional exchange of blows like what happened between Asimov and Heinlein.

That wasn't the first fight at the convention, not by a long shot. Some of the more politically active members of the convention took part in the weekend anti-war protests down in Berkeley. There were a lot of bloodied people, though—truth to tell—most of the casualties came from the fire escape.

See, the Clarion Hotel had a fire escape which was actually nothing more than a circular slide at the end of the building, with openings on each floor. Fans took the towels from their rooms and slid down on them all night long. There were lots of collisions and tangled bodies.

It was a lot of fun, especially late at night after taking a couple of those aspirin Jerry Phipps was passing out like candy. Some people even carried sparklers and incense on the way down. There were a couple of small fires and a well-known writer broke his leg, but nothing really bad happened. Some say that the idea for the Space Mountain ride at Disney was born that weekend. I don't doubt it.

But I digress. You want to hear about what happened at the banquet. That was when Asimov and Heinlein duked it out and, in the minds of many, totally destroyed SFWA.

Of course, there are those who hold that the Science Fiction Writers of America, as it was known then, was ripe for the toppling, being an organization deeply bogged down in membership qualification squabbles and an endless debate on the design for the SFWA tie.

I disagree. SFWA has done many useful things for its membership over the years. Besides, I kind of like the idea of a tie. A tasteful dark blue would be nice, perhaps with little rocket ships. I would definitely vote against that ugly red design some fashion-impaired people would like to see us saddled with.

But I digress. Let me return to the banquet.

At Baycon they still had a formal banquet. To tell you the truth, I don't miss them much. They tried to squeeze everything into one

112

big affair: Hugo Awards, Guest of Honor speeches, Big Heart Award. Everything.

And the food. It was awful. Luke-warm rubber chicken, roast beef you could gnaw on for a week, congealed gravy, a wilted lettuce salad, some sort of a green vegetable sliding off the plate. Weak coffee, cold of course, and a piece of cake you could use for a hockey puck. I don't know how hotels get away with serving food like that. It ought to be against the law, that's what I think. Here we are, a captured audience and they force us to eat swill they'd be ashamed to serve in the state prison.

I could go on about food, which is almost as much fun to talk about as sex, but I see Tony giving me the "five minute" sign, so I'd better wrap this up. Pass me another beer, would you? Where was I?

Ah, yes. The banquet. The Big Feud came to a head during Philip Jose Farmer's Guest of Honor speech. Of course a lot of things had time to happen during that speech, which was slightly longer than your average major league baseball game.

Now it wasn't Phil's fault. He had a theme, and a decent one at that. I place the major blame on the hotel, which had come out about fifty dinners short. Nothing like a lack of food to get people a bit testy during a five hour speech. They ran out of coffee, too, which is unacceptable and probably a breach of contract. A hotel should never run out of coffee. Sooner they should run out of ice than coffee. Or maybe those suspect vegetables.

Right, Tony. Three minutes. Got it.

As I recall, Phil's speech had to do with morality. It tied the war protests outside the hotel to literature and a writer's obligation to do something or say something or at least write about something. Yeah, it went like that, more or less.

Writers should write something. Good advice.

If I had expected a fight that night, I would not have predicted it would be between two of our elder statesmen, unless maybe it involved Lester del Rey. Or Damon Knight, if the dispute was over punctuation. Well, Harlan is always a possibility. Ted White, maybe. Come to think of it, the list of possibilities is pretty long. But Heinlein and Asimov? No way.

But it happened. As real as I'm sitting here before you. I saw it with my own eyes.

113

You see, we not only had Hawks and Doves, we also had Spock.

The outside world had the baby doctor turned pacifist, but we had the Spock with pointy ears. And we didn't know what to do with him.

I suppose this seems old now, what with *Star Trek: The Thirty-seventh Generation* already in reruns, but back then we were presented with a dilemma. *Star Trek* could be kind of hokey at times, but it *did* occasionally use authentic science fiction writers. Once in a while, a real good episode would come on the tube. Lots of people watched the show. Would they think this was all there was to science fiction? Would we be buried by Trek fans, some of which had never read an actual book? It was a conundrum.

A conundrum is a question or problem having only a conjectural answer. Who would have thought it would be settled, once and for all, by a fist fight at a Worldcon banquet?

Without a doubt, *Star Trek* could not be compared with such classics as "The Demolished Man." On the other hand, it was not *Lost in Space*, either. Science Fiction Fandom had always prided itself with being open and accepting. Would the fans we welcomed end up taking over? It was a real fear among some of the old guard.

Tradition is everything; without it we are rootless, adrift in the sea of time without a compass. But sometimes tradition can be a wall, a blind spot to keep us from seeing change. One great science fiction tradition is feuds.

We've had our share of feuds, running back to the beginning of time. I hear H.G. Wells even feuded with Jules Verne back in the real old days. And we haven't even gotten to Ted White yet, who feuded with nearly everyone at one time or another.

And tempers. Wow, we had tempers. Still do, as a matter of fact. Science fiction seems to attract people with passion, both as readers and as writers.

This passion caused Isaac Asimov to break a long-standing vow and drive across the country for a convention.

This passion caused Robert Heinlein, who had been a virtual hermit for years, to surface at a Worldcon.

And what drove these men to such lengths? I can sum it up in one word: *Star Trek*.

What I didn't know at the time, being a mere fan and not privy to the inner workings of SFWA, was that the organization was split down the middle on a matter of great import. Half the organization felt that *Star Trek* novels should not be accepted as qualifications for membership. The other half felt that *only Star Trek* novels should qualify someone for membership.

It came to that.

About four hours into Phil's speech, he paused for a sip of water. Asimov, always the opportunist, seized this opportunity to jump to his feet and shout his views to the assembled multitude.

Heinlein, the consummate gentleman, then rose in his chair and rebutted Asimov, point for point. He then threw a piece of petrified hotel cake at the Good Doctor, opening a scalp wound that bled a surprisingly large amount.

Harlan and Lester tried in vain to stop the fight from getting any worse. Ted Cogswell shouted encouragement to both combatants. Damon Knight threw peanut shells at everyone.

When the dust settled and the peanut shells quit flying it had been decided. The rest, as they say, is history.

Thank you very much. I hope to speak to you again at Noreascon 13.

Author, critic, deaf gossip columnist, and former keeper of Her Majesty's Own Nuclear Deterrent, David Langford has won more Hugo Awards than God. An individual who plays, not incidentally, no small part in what follows.

—P.N.H.

THE SPEAR OF THE SUN
David Langford

Since its inception in 1925, the most famous shared-world series in *G.K.Chesterton's Science Fiction Magazine* has always been the adventures of that much-loved interplanetary sleuth Father (later in the chronology, Monsignor) Brown. There is no need to list the long roll-call of those who have taken part—Hilaire Belloc, Graham Greene, Jorge Luis Borges, Kurt Scheer, Clark Darlton, R. A. Lafferty and Robert Lionel Fanthorpe being just a few of the illustrious contributors[1], not to mention the bright talents emerging from the splendid *GKC Presents Catholic Writers of the Future* anthologies—and we are always glad to welcome fresh participants. Here, therefore, is the first of *GKSFM's* eagerly awaited new series "The Fractals of Father Brown," penned by SF Achievement ("Gilbert") Award-winner David Langford. . . .

The Spear of the Sun

The luxury liner *H.M.S. Aquinas* sped among the stars, its great engines devouring distance and defying time. Each porthole offered a lurid glimpse of that colossal pointillist work which God Himself has painted in subtle yet searing star-points upon the black canvas of creation, too vast for any critic ever to step back and see entire. In the main lounge, however, the ship's passengers were already jaded

---

1   We remind our readers that Mr Philip José Farmer's delightful but unauthorized contributions (*Father Brown vs the Insidious Dr Fu-Manchu, Father Brown 124C41+, Father Brown in Oz*, etc) are not regarded as strictly canonical.

by the splendour of the suns and had found a new distraction. For Astron, high celebrant of the newest religion, was weaving dazzling circles of rhetoric around a shabby, blinking priest of the oldest.

"Did not a great writer once say that the interstellar spaces are God's quarantine regulations? I think the blight He had in mind was the blight of men like this, crabbed and joyless celibates who spread their poisoned doctrines of guilt and fear from planet to planet, world after world growing grey with their breath. . . ."

The crabbed and joyless object of these attentions sipped wine and contrived to look remarkably cheerful. Father Brown was travelling from his parish of Cobhole in England on Old Earth as an emissary to the colony world Pavonia III, where Astron planned to harvest countless converts and (it is to be assumed) decidedly countable cash donations for his Universal Temple of Fire.

"For the Church of Fire pays heed to its handmaid Science, and sheds the mouldy baggage of superstition. The living Church of Fire gives respect to the atomic blaze at the heart of every sun, to the divine laws of supersymmetry and chaos theory; the dying church of superstition had nothing to say about either at Vatican III."

The little, pudding-faced priest murmured: "We never needed chaos theory to know that the cycles of evil run ever smaller and smaller down the scales of measurement, yet always dreadfully self-similar." But it passed unheeded.

Astron boomed on, remarking that those who obstructed the universal Light would be struck down by the spear of the sun. Indeed he looked every inch the pagan god, with his great height, craggy features and flowing flaxen hair now streaked with silver. A golden sunburst of a ring gleamed on his finger. His acolyte Simon Traill was yet more handsome though less vocal, perhaps a little embarrassed at Astron's taunting. Both wore plain robes of purest white. The group that pressed around consisted chiefly of women; Father Brown noted with interest that red-haired Elizabeth Brayne, whom he knew to be the billionaire heiress of Brayne Interplanetary, pressed closest of all and close in particular to young Traill. She wore the dangerous look of a woman who thinks she knows her own mind.

"Damn them," said a voice at Brown's ear. "Pardon me, Father. But you heard that Astron saying what he thinks of celibacy. He chews women up and spits out the pieces. See Signora Maroni back

117

there with a face like thunder? She's a bit long in the tooth for Mr Precious Astron, but for the first two nights of this trip she had something he wanted. Now that something's in his blasted Temple fund, and—Well, perhaps you wouldn't understand."

"Oh, stories like this do occasionally crop up in the confessional," said the dumpling-faced priest vaguely, eyeing the dark young man. John Horne was a mining engineer, who until now had talked of nothing but Pavonia III's bauxite and the cargo of advanced survey and digging equipment that was travelling out with him. Father Brown knew the generous wrath of simple men, and tried to spread a little calm by enquiring about the space-walk in which several of the passengers had indulged earlier.

Though allowing himself to be diverted for a little time, Horne presently said, "Don't you feel a shade hot under the dog-collar when Astron needles you about his Religion of Science and how outdated you are?"

"Oh yes, science progresses most remarkably," said Father Brown with bumbling enthusiasm. "In Sir Isaac Newton's mechanics, you know, it was the three-body problem that didn't have any general solution. Then came Relativity and it was the two-body problem that was troublesome. After that, Quantum Theory found all these complications in the *one*-body problem, a single particle; and now they tell me that relativistic quantum field theory is stuck at the no-body problem, the vacuum itself. I can hardly wait to hear what tremendous step comes next."

Horne looked at him a little uncertainly.

A silvery chime sounded. "Attention, attention. This is the captain speaking. Dinner will be served at six bells. Shortly beforehand there will be a course correction with a temporary boost of acceleration from five-eighths to fifteen-sixteenths g."

"I go," said Astron with a kind of stately anger, drawing himself up to his full, impressive height and pulling the deep white cowl of the robe over his head. "I go to be alone and meditate over the Sacred Flame." With Traill cowled likewise in his wake, he stalked gigantically from the lounge.

"That makes me madder than anything," Horne said gloomily, beginning to amble in the general direction of Elizabeth Brayne. "No pipes, no cigarettes, that's an iron rule—and *he* manages to wangle an

118

eternal flame in his ruddy stateroom. The safety officer would like to kill him."

But it was not the safety officer who came under suspicion when the news raced through the *Aquinas* like leaves in a mad March wind: that a third lieutenant making final checks before the course change had used a master key and found that great robed figure slumped over the brazier of the Universal Flame, face charred and flowing hair gone to smoke, a scientific seeker who had solved the no-body problem at last.

By a happy chance, ship security had been contracted out to the agency of M. Hercule Flambeau[2], one-time master criminal and an old friend of Father Brown, who set to in a frenzy of Gallic fervour. Knowing the little priest's power of insight, Flambeau invited him at once to the chamber of death. It was a stark and austere stateroom, distinguished by the wide brazier (its gas flame now extinguished) and the terrible figure that the third lieutenant had pulled from the fire.

"He seems to have bent over his wretched flame and prayed, or whatever mumbo-jumbo the cult of Fire uses for prayer," mused Father Brown. "Better for him to have looked up and not down, and savoured the stars through that porthole. . . . Even the stars look twisted in this accursed place. Might he have died naturally and fallen? That would be ugly enough, but not devilish."

The tall Flambeau drew out a slip of computer paper. "My friend, we know to distrust coincidence. The acolyte Traill is nowhere to be found, and the ship's records say the nearest airlock has cycled just once, outwards, since Astron left the main lounge an hour ago. Some avenger has made a clean sweep of the Church of Fire's mission: one dead in a locked room, one jettisoned. And half the women and all the men out there might have had a potent motive. We're carrying members of rival cults too—the Club of Queer Trades, the Dead Men's Shoes Society, the Ten Teacups, and heaven knows what else. But how

---

2   Flambeau repented, made his full confession to Father Brown, and joined the side of the angels on some 42 occasions, all listed in Martin Gardner's *Flambeau, Boskone and Ming the Merciless: the Annotated Father Brown Villains* (1987).

in God's name could any of them get in here?"

"Don't forget the crabbed priesthood that blights human souls," said the smaller man earnestly. "Astron was last seen attacking it with a will, and its representative has an obviously criminal face. *Ecce homo.*" He tapped himself on the chest.

"Father Brown, I cannot believe you did this thing."

"Well, in confidence, I'll admit to you that I didn't." He bustled curiously about the room, blinking at the oversized bed and peering again through the viewport as though the stars themselves held some elusive clue. Last of all he studied the robed corpse's ruined face and pale hands, and shuddered.

"The spear of the sun," he muttered to himself. "Astron threatened his enemies with the spear of the sun. And where does a wise man hide a spear?"

"In an armoury, I suppose," said Flambeau in a low voice.

"In William Blake's armoury. You remember, *All the stars threw down their spears?* But the angel Ithuriel also carries a spear. Excuse me, I know I'm rambling, but I can see half of it, just half. . . ." Father Brown stood stock still with fingers pressed into his screwed-up eyes. At last he said: "You thought I shuddered at that wreck of a face. I shuddered at the hands."

"But there is nothing to see—no mark on the hands."

"There is nothing. And there should be a great sunburst ring. They are younger hands than Astron's, when you look. It is the acolyte Traill who lies there."

Flambeau gaped. "But that can't be. It turns everything topsy-turvy; it makes the whole case the wrong shape."

"So was that equation," said Father Brown gently. "And we survived even that equation.[3] But I need one further fact." He scribbled on a slip of paper and folded it. "Have one of your men show this to John Horne. A reply is expected."

---

3   Older readers will recognize the allusion to that insight which saved the Holy Galactic Empire from the threat of secular "psychohistorians" in Isaac Asimov's classic *Foundation and Father Brown* (1951).

Wordlessly, Flambeau pressed a stud and did what was asked. "Horne," he said when the two friends were alone again. "The one who fancies Miss Brayne and didn't like her interest in men with white robes. Is he your choice for the dock?"

"No. For the witness-box." Father Brown sat on the edge of the bed, the dinginess of his cassock highlighted by the expanse of white satin quilting, his stubby legs not quite reaching the deck plates. "I think this story begins with young Horne prattling over dinner about his cargo. So I asked whether a piece of his equipment was missing. Come now: when you think of fiery death in a locked stateroom, what does mining and surveying gear suggest to you?"

"Nothing but moonshine," said Flambeau with sarcasm. "I do assure you that each hull plate and bulkhead has been carefully inspected for any trace of a four-foot mineshaft through which a murderer might crawl."

"That's the whole sad story. Even when you look at it you can't see it: but every stateroom of this vessel contains a Judas window through which death can strike. And—" Brown's muddy eyes widened suddenly. "Of course! The spear of the sun is two-edged. My friend, I predict . . . I predict that you will never make an arrest."

As Flambeau arose with an oath, the communicator on his wrist crackled. "What? The answer is yes? Father, the answer is yes."

"Then let me tell you the story," said the priest. "The great Astron devoured woman after woman, but most of all he craved the women who did not crave him. For as I saw, Elizabeth Brayne was taken with Simon Traill. And Astron left the room in anger.

"I fancy it was his practice to have Traill watch over the ritual flame for him, while another cowled figure glided out upon certain assignations. But this time Astron's assignation was a darker one. He knew where to find the pressure suits: there was a space-walking party a few watches ago. He knew that in Horne's cargo he would find his spear."

"Which is—?"

"A laser."

Father Brown continued dreamily after a sort of thunderous silence. "Picture Astron floating a little way outside that porthole, a wide-open window for his frightful, insubstantial bolt. Picture his unknowing rival Traill bent over the flame, struck in the face, falling dead across the brazier which would slowly burn away every mark of how he died."

"Name of a name," cried Flambeau. "He is still out there. We shall have him yet!"

"You will never have him." Father Brown shook his head slowly. "The spear, I said, is two-edged. Oh, these strong and simple Stoics with their great bold ideas! Astron called us impractical and superstitious, but lacked even the little smattering of quantum electrodynamics that every seminarian picks up along with his Latin and his St. Augustine. He thought the crystal of the port purely transparent, Flambeau: but there is diffraction, my friend, and there is partial reflection. And even as it slew his victim, the spear of the sun rebounded to strike the murderer blind." The little priest shivered. "Yes, the humour of God can be cruel. Astron's easy arrogance saw the motes in all men's eyes, and now at last found the beam in his own. . . .

"Picture him now, flinging his suit this way and that with those clever little gas-jets, with nightmare pressing in as he realizes he *cannot find the ship* in the endless dark. And then comes the course correction and he has no more chance. And now that void which he worshipped in his heart has become his vast sarcophagus."

"I think," said Flambeau slowly, "that brandy would be a good thing. Mother of God. All that from a missing ring."

"Not only that." said Father Brown, "The viewport crystal was slightly distorted by the heat of the beam's passage. I said the stars looked twisted, but you thought I was being sentimental."

———

IN OUR NEXT ISSUE: Fr. Brian Stableford continues his series on forgotten sf authors, with a spirited case for reviving the works of nineteenth-century fantasist H.G.Wells. Our regular *Credo Quia Impossibile* squib daringly tackles another zero-probability notion in "The Piltdown Effect"—we know from *GKSFM* science columns by Hilaire Belloc, Jimmy Swaggart and other fine popularizers that mankind is a fixed genetic type, *but just suppose for one terrifying moment that it were not so!* Of course the "Should Women Authors Be Allowed In *GKSFM?*" debate rages on in the letter column: what amusingly outrageous thing *will* that "Ms" Cadigan say next? Carl Sagan contributes a devastatingly frank essay on science's inability to explain weeping images or miraculous liquefactions. And our millions of avid readers in the Americas will welcome the coming feature on brash colonial editor Gardner Dozois and his shoestring launch of (at last!) an all-United States sf magazine, called *Interzone*: we shall have to look to our laurels. . . .

www.ingramcontent.com/pod-product-compliance
Lightning Source LLC
Chambersburg PA
CBHW030145200626
46812CB00015B/1696